Terror-Dot-Gov

Docufictions
by Harold Jaffe

Published by Raw Dog Screaming Press
Hyattsville, MD

First paperback edition

Cover image & Interior illustrations: Katana Blue
Book design: Jennifer C. Barnes
Author photo: Gayle Luque

Printed in the United States of America

ISBN: 1-933293-09-8

Library of Congress Control Number: 2005902917

www.rawdogscreaming.com

Acknowledgements

A number of these "docufictions" were published in the following journals and anthologies: *Submodern*; *Obscure Publications*; *Denver Quarterly*; *Journal of Experimental Fiction*; *Locus/Novus*; *Crown of Bones*; *Sunshine/Noir*; *Shincho* (Japan); *Fiction International*.

I'd like to thank Lawrence-Minh Bui Davis, Andrew Koopmans, Stephen-Paul Martin and Gayle Luque for reading and commenting on this volume in manuscript.

Critical Response to Harold Jaffe's Fiction

15 Serial Killers
"With this latest salvo of guerrilla writing, Harold Jaffe explodes the very social, political, and narrative structures supporting capitalist culture's illusory edifices, further cementing his reputation as one of our finest literary terrorists/freedom fighters." —Paradoxa

False Positive
"These short treats transform 15 news vignettes into gruesomely interesting oddities...Jaffe is a master at illuminating our culture's most evasive grotesqueries." —San Francisco Chronicle

Sex for the Millennium
"Something's going on here, low-key, cool, and disturbing. These subtle displacements of desire fix to your memory, and, with their humor and pathos, gnaw there a long time." —Samuel R. Delany

Straight Razor
"As technically outrageous and emotionally intense as a madman's shotgun held to the temple of contemporary culture. [Jaffe's 12 stories] succeed terrifically." —Review of Contemporary Fiction

Othello Blues
"Composed almost wholly of stage directions, quick cuts, and dialogue, Jaffe's novel is an imaginative, witty, and politically prescient retelling of Othello." —Thomas LeClair

Eros Anti-Eros
"Jaffe's fictions are a wonder of deadpan humor, biting wit, and visual beauty. No recent fiction has gripped me with such force and immediacy. —Marianne Hauser

Madonna and Other Spectacles
"Crackling with rage and black laughter, these fictions wrench themselves out of the grimmest facts: genocide, nuclear devastation, black poverty, corporate murder. [This is] a collection that confronts terror in street language and redoubles its impact." —Publisher's Weekly

Beasts
"Jaffe's convincing portraits of the dispossessed are moving, insightful glimpses of the human spirit under stress." —The New York Times Book Review

Dos Indios
"Told with the simplicity of a folk tale, this spiritual journey of a Peruvian flute player is a beautiful and moving story." —Newsday

Books by Harold Jaffe

Terror-Dot-Gov (docufictions; visuals by Katana Blue)
15 Serial Killers (docufictions; visuals by Joel Lipman)
False Positive (fictions)
Sex for the Millennium (extreme tales)
Straight Razor (stories; visuals by Norman Conquest)
Othello Blues (novel)
Eros Anti-Eros (fictions)
Madonna and Other Spectacles (fictions)
Beasts (fictions)
Dos Indios (novel)
Mourning Crazy Horse (stories)
Mole's Pity (novel)

Note

Terror-Dot-Gov marks an extension of a project begun with False Positive (2002) and continued with 15 Serial Killers (2003), namely to create fiction out of "information," especially information which professes to be news.

Employing various stratagems, I treat selected news items, attempting to tease out their often conflicting subtexts.

In the previous two volumes I mostly addressed "news" of the dark side and extremity.

In Terror-Dot-Gov, I have turned my attention specifically to war and "terrorism."

The resultant texts I've called "docufictions."

Contents

for the actual victims of terror

You make a desert and call it peace

—Tacitus

Behead

The head of Brent Marshall was discovered in a refrigerator during a police raid on an apartment in the Saudi capital Riyadh, the interior ministry reported.

A large man said to weigh more than 300 pounds, Marshall was abducted by an Al-Qaeda cell on 12 June.

Marshall, from Dungannon, Virginia, had been reportedly working as a helicopter gunship engineer in Saudi Arabia for US defense contractor Lockheed Martin.

In the apartment where Marshall's head was discovered, Saudi security forces also found a surface-to-air missile, rocket-propelled grenades, automatic rifles, semi-automatic pistols, lap-top computers, credit cards, nitrates, prayer beads, a monopoly set in Arabic, and an empty prescription container of the anti-depressant Zoloft.

The discoveries were made after Saudi police stormed the apartment, killing two suspected militants, the interior ministry reported. It said three other militants were apprehended after being injured in the attack.

The raid in the capital's King Fahd District also led to the arrest of the wife and six children of Al-Qaeda's local chief, Saleh al-Oufi, officials said. It is not known if Oufi himself was involved in the fighting, which is said to have started when security forces investigating the property came under fire.

If Oufi is found guilty in absentia his wife and six children can be lawfully beheaded.

A former government minister, Oufi became Al-Qaeda's Saudi Arabia chief after the death of his predecessor, Abdul Aziz al-Muqrin.

Muqrin was reportedly killed in a shoot-out with security forces, sparked by the sighting of a black Mercedes sedan filled with militants parked by a reservoir attempting to dispose of a very large corpse, thought to have been that of the beheaded Brent Marshall.

According to Saudi security forces, as he was about to be killed in a hail of gunfire, Muqrin raised his head to the sky and shouted: "I have fulfilled my vow to Allah."

The Saudi interior minister later reported that Brent Marshall's headless body was not the corpse in question and had in fact not yet been found.

Marshall's family in Dungannon, Virginia, appealed to US authorities to pressure the Saudi government to end the confusion surrounding the body.

Militants appeared on a video in June with a blindfolded Marshall wearing a very large version of the orange jumpsuit that American captors force Muslim inmates to wear in the high security facility in Guantánamo Bay. The militants demanded that Saudi Arabia release all prisoners arrested because of their alleged connections with militant Muslim organizations.

After the deadline for their demands passed, graphic, grainy images of the massive American's beheading were displayed on a website linked to Muslim militants, as well as on Al-Jazeera, the pan-Arab online news network.

Because of Marshall's exceptionally thick neck, the masked executioner in his black jubbah with his long curved blade seemed to have trouble severing the head. In any event, he made a messy business of it.

Marshall was the second US civilian to have been beheaded by his abductors in the region this year.

G. Gordon Slade, a medium-sized US businessman in Iraq, allegedly associated with the CIA, was shown being beheaded by a masked militant in a black jubbah on a website linked to Islamic causes.

A CIA spokesperson in Kuwait City officially denied any association with G. Gordon Slade.

Numerous other civilians, many of them aid workers from countries around the globe, have been abducted and either beheaded or almost beheaded.

Fareeda Azza Khan, diplomatic affairs correspondent of the daily Indian newspaper *The Hindu*, was the latest to be almost beheaded. She was finally freed, she claimed, less because she was female than because she was Muslim.

In point of fact Fareeda Azza Khan is not Muslim but a Parsee orphan adopted as an infant by Muslim parents in the city of Hyderabad in Andhra Pradesh state. Her biological parents were allegedly murdered by the Tamil Tigers, a Hindu guerrilla army from in and around Madras who have been warring against the Sinhalese Buddhist majority in Sri Lanka for the last three decades.

Ms Khan, 29, was the seventh foreign woman taken in the flood of kidnappings that have swept Iraq and other Middle East regions since the US-led coalition's liberation of Iraq.

Fareeda Azza Khan wrote the account of her grueling abduction and near-beheading in the Sunday magazine supplement of *The Hindu* (www.hinduonnet.com). From the start, she reported, her captors made her dress in a long loose coat and tied a scarf, or hijab, over her head. They did not wish to look at her in her jeans and pink T-shirt with the small green Mobil Oil logo above her left breast.

Which is the opposite of what American captors did to their Muslim prisoners in Abu Ghraib, forcing them to strip naked before abusing them.

"Look how beautiful you look," the Muslim abductors cooed, and Fareeda Azza Khan would weep at her veiled reflection in the mirror. "It was not me," she said. "I was losing me."

Almost immediately after her abduction she was shuffled from captor to captor.

Everywhere she was taken, she said, people, ordinary Iraqis, appeared eager to help the "resistance." The abductors even used Iraqi children to bring them water, but nobody treated them like children. They'd be standing guard while the men talked about severing heads, "so you became afraid of the children too."

Finally, after six days (she made a point of keeping a precise record of the time), Ms Khan stopped being shuffled about and was kept bound and usually blindfolded on the outskirts of the northern Iraq city of Mosul.

Her abductors identified themselves as members of Ansar al-Islam, a fundamentalist Muslim group that according to US intelligence had set up several Taliban-like enclaves in central and northern Iraq before the war.

US authorities have officially linked the group to Al-Qaeda and Abu Musab al-Zarqawi, the Jordanian-born terrorist who has recently supplanted Osama bin Laden as *numero uno* on the US Most Wanted list.

Fareeda Azza Khan wrote in *The Hindu* that the apparent leader of her abductors, whom the others referred to as Emir, "removed the blindfold tied very tightly around my head. He sat down on a cushion on the filthy floor across from me and stared intensely into my eyes. He spoke softly in Arabic.

"'Please understand why we have to make sure who you are. There have been many spies here, and we had to cut their heads off.'"

Spy Fareeda Azza Khan explained, referred to any "kaffir" or "infidel." For the abductors, there was evidently no difference between a Christian and a Jew, a white European and an American.

"'I would like to talk to you, Muslim to Muslim,' the emir said to the abducted journalist. 'When you cry, you break my heart. But if you scream, I will have to be cruel to you.'"

Although Fareeda Azza Khan's name indicated that she shared their religion, the militants considered her too independent to be a Muslim woman except in name.

Neither her sex nor her name saved her from being severely beaten and constantly threatened with beheading. Once, after yet another accusation, she shouted back: "I came here for you, to get your side of the story, so I've got no words to say to people like you."

"That was when they got really angry," she continued in her account for *The Hindu*. "But you know, that was the real me."

After her outburst, the Arab terrorists wrapped a red and white scarf around her face so tightly that she thought she would go blind. They led her outside and started beating her with straps and chains. It was only then, she said, that she realized how numb she had become.

"I know it sounds strange," she wrote in *The Hindu*, "but I was happy at that moment because at least I could feel my body. I felt like I was coming back to myself. Until then, I couldn't make eye contact. Everybody kept leering at me and making that cutting sign across their throat."

Horrifying as her abduction was, it gave her, she recounted in her article in *The Hindu*, a close-up view of the kidnappers' fascination with death, their view of Islam and the links between ethnically diverse insurgents in northern Iraq.

"These people think they are living in the time of the Crusades," Fareeda Azza Khan explained. "They say they are fighting for Islam first and Iraq second. They are absolutely certain that their religion is being attacked from all sides by infidels led by the Americans and Zionists."

After the final beating, she was left bleeding and semi-conscious on the hard, bullet-scarred ground outside the abductors' hovel. Someone had removed the scarf around her eyes. Her torturers were gone.

She was free.

Fareeda Azza Khan was initially abducted after she took a taxi from the makeshift airport south to Mosul. When the taxi stopped allegedly to ask a policeman to direct them, the policeman waved over a fire engine-red Ford Explorer with three masked men inside who ordered Ms. Khan to get in.

She was blindfolded and taken to a nondescript house, unaware of what lay ahead.

As of this writing, the beheadings of kidnapped civilians in the Middle East, notably in Iraq, total 311. Which is still many fewer than the estimated 12,000 guillotined French who found themselves on the wrong side of the revolution.

That was of course centuries ago. Moreover, the French executioners were employing the most advanced technology available at the time.

Pizza Cannibal

He was a 43-year-old bachelor who shared a cramped studio apartment with a cockatiel and two hamsters, slept on his couch, and ate warmed-over pizza for breakfast, while watching NFL football or Rush Limbaugh on the small-screen Mitsubishi with the sound muted.

Thin and stooped, he was shy with adults but animated with adolescent boys and animals, the sort who would get on all fours to play with a neighbor's pet tarantula.

He wore his jeans above his navel and frayed white dress shirt buttoned all the way up his neck without a tie.

If Seldon "Salt" Brumley, was something of a loner with stooped shoulders, large flat feet, stick-out ears, and John Lennon-style granny glasses, he was also unfailingly polite and soft-spoken, acquaintances recalled.

It could be that he was soft-spoken because of his cleft palate which had been operated on unsuccessfully when he was a child in the outer reaches of New Jersey.

Nobody, including his mother, seemed to know how he acquired the odd nickname, Salt.

Softly, Salt would talk with the young males in their tank tops who looked under the hoods of their cars and pickups while sipping Coors from the bottle.

They'd talk about Rush Limbaugh, the terrorist threat from the Muslim sector, Extreme Games, and the Marine Corps.

Surprisingly, Salt did a lot of the talking, and it could be that the cocky, gender-fast young males didn't really listen to him.

But they didn't dismiss him out of hand either.

They didn't kick his ass or snuff out cigarette butts on his neck.

They didn't dress up in cop unis and sodomize him with a broomstick.

One Sunday a month, and two on leap year, Salt Brumley would invite his widowed mother Sally over for vodka martinis, chicken fried steak and a TV movie.

Actually, Salt drank a sweetish rosé with his steak.

But it was double martinis for Sally, always with three anchovy olives, which Salt had to buy in a specialty shop on the other side of town.

The last movie they saw, according to Sally Brumley, was that old one with James Stewart and Grace Kelly, *Rear Window.*

So just who was Seldon "Salt" Brumley, the pizza deliveryman at the center of one of the top six strangest suspense stories of the year?

Last Monday at 11:33 a.m., Brumley, rolling a small dolly, walked into a Bank of America branch on Lumumba, four blocks from Vito's Pizza Parlor where he worked, opened up his frayed white dress shirt to show a bomb attached to his neck, and demanded cash.

The bank teller who knew Salt, as everyone knew each other in the small all-American town, smiled warmly while pressing the silent buzzer to alert the police.

Rolling three canvas bags of marked bills and another bag of quarters on the dolly, Salt climbed into his pizza delivery van.

He didn't get far: two CHP cops on their Harleys, one with red hair and freckles, the other Latino, with a gleaming smile and hyper-macho manner, pulled him over a few hundred feet from the bank parking lot.

But as the motorcycle cops waited for the bomb squad to arrive, the device around Salt Brumley's neck exploded, blasting a cellphone-size hole in his chest.

Raining blood over the pigs straddling their hogs.

Salt Brumley bled to death sitting cross-legged in the street.

Before he died Brumley told the cops that a dark-skinned man with a strange accent whose breath smelled of hummus attached the bomb to his neck, clicking it closed with a red Masters-brand combination lock that seemed to set a timer.

Brumley said the dark-skinned man, who wore a black turban and orange, ankle-length, sheet-like garment, instructed him to rob the Bank of America branch on Lumumba and return to an address south of the city with the $$$.

Only then would the bomb be defused and removed from his neck.

Now the feds are trying to figure out what, if anything, is true about Salt Brumley's story.

Was he, as he said, the unwilling victim of a Muslim terrorist conspiracy that miscarried?

Was Brumley himself a Muslim convert who acted alone?

Was he coerced into a terror-suicide mission?

Was he for whatever reason employing an elaborate method to commit suicide on his own?

To the handful of humans who claimed to know Salt Brumley in this aging industrial city of 89,000 along Lake Erie, the answer is clear.

No way, they contend, could this childlike (read: moronic) pale male have concocted, much less carried out, such an elaborate scheme.

Nor was he in any way, shape or form suicidal.

On the contrary, he loved life, loved his job, and was proud to be an American.

Either terrorists forced him to commit the crime or humans he trusted duped him into acting as an accomplice.

"Salt's the last person you'd imagine being part of this kind of crime conspiracy," said Johnny Polar, 41, who lived next door to Brumley on a working-class street lined with 1950s-era tract homes, most of them sub-divided for rentals, in Mitchell, a suburb east of Sioux Falls.

"It just don't add up."

Polar's 15-year-old son, JJ, balanced on his skateboard while talking on his cellphone, interjected, "He was way too dumb."

Salt Brumley dropped out of high school in his sophomore year, had a hard time changing the tire on his pizza delivery vehicle and didn't own either a computer or a cellphone.

No one who knew him believed he had the skills to make a crude bomb, much less make the metal collar locking the device to his neck, which the feds say was sophisticated.

The feds say they have only seen a few of these collar bombs in the US, and that was in San Francisco during the time of ACT-UP, the violent homosexual AIDS-terrorist conspiracy in the late 1980s and early '90s.

However, insurgents in Yemen, the Palestine territories and cocaine-ridden Colombia have commonly used the collar bomb devices equipped with remote-control detonators.

Though light years from being well off, Salt Brumley never showed any interest in material acquisition, living just above the poverty line with no complaints, according to acquaintances.

Of course, it wouldn't have been easy for the homely bachelor with the stick-out ears, large flat feet, cleft palate, and low IQ to have been other than poor.

After his Ford Pinto was wrecked in an accident and he had no way to deliver pizzas, he confided to his landlady, Madge Hrbek, that he would rather go jobless and homeless than move in with his mother

The landlady helped him buy a used, red, white and blue GMC van for $1,135, which Salt was repaying in $108 per month installments.

He had fully repaid the loan just four days before he died.

"He was real proud," said Mrs. Hrbek, who had rented the cramped studio to Brumley for nearly six years.

"He'd never accept the food we offered him, except maybe a cookie.

"He loved tollhouse cookies.

"The real kind, crisp and filled to the brim with chocolate chips.

"Milk chocolate, not bittersweet."

Seldon Brumley was born and raised in the tiny hamlet of Kellogg, Iowa, one of at least five children, investigators said.

His father died of prostate cancer about a decade ago.

His mother, who lives just east of Cedar Rapids, claimed to have lost touch with all of her children but Salt.

Well, one of them died of crib death and another was killed in the first Gulf war.

Which left three, including Salt, and of those three, Shep was serving time in Attica State Prison for armed robbery.

Shep never admitted his guilt, and 12 years after his imprisonment his court-appointed lawyer produced DNA evidence that exonerated him.

When he was let out, without compensation, he disappeared, prison tattoos up and down his body.

In his freshman year at Desert Oriole High School, in Needles, California, records show that Seldon Salt Brumley failed algebra and Spanish, got D's in Composition, Biology, and Home Economics, and earned an A- in Motorcross.

The records show that he attended only 23 days of school in his sophomore year before dropping out to go to work.

Though neighbors and investigators knew little about his early work history, evidently Salt Brumley spent the past dozen years, and maybe longer, delivering pizzas.

About two-and-a-half years ago, Brumley moved to Prescott, Arizona, to live with a younger sister, Sarah, and work at her tool and die shop, Madge Hrbek, his landlady, informed the feds.

He got rid of most of his belongings, expecting never to return.

But he was back at her doorstep seven months later, Mrs. Hrbek said.

She never asked him what happened in Prescott, Arizona, and he never volunteered.

One theory is that Salt fell in with terrorists and suicide bombers, and converted to Muslim in Prescott, Arizona.

His last day on this sweet earth began like most others.

Salt Brumley got up at 6:30 a.m. and fed his hamsters and his cockatiel.

Then he swallowed three antacid tablets.

Then he picked up the daily newspaper outside his door and drove to Wendy's where he ordered his usual breakfast.

Eggs Benedict, home fries, and a double vanilla latte.

Then he drove to work at Vito's Pizza Parlor, a hole-in-the-wall restaurant that shares space with a swing dance studio, Korean massage parlor, cellular phone store, and herbal products shop, in a miniature strip mall on busy Dogstar Street.

Just after 1:30, feds say, the pizza shop owner, Vito Pontecorvo, took an order for two anchovy, cheese, sausage, red pepper and pineapple pizzas.

The caller claimed to be the manager of an Internet café on Biko Street.

Vito said he heard belly dancing-type Middle Eastern music in the background and thought maybe he could smell some hummus over the phone.

The Biko Street address turned out to be a weeping birch tree by the west bank of the Hillsdale Creek.

Above the creek was a white cinder-block building on top of which was a transmission tower belonging to a local FOX affiliate.

It is not clear if Salt Brumley ever reached the FOX transmission tower.

What is known is that around 2:30 he showed up at the Bank of America branch on Lumumba with the bomb around his neck, a small dolly under his arm, and a note for the teller.

The feds say the handwriting is being analyzed.

Salt, with the four canvas bags of marked bills and one bag of quarters on the passenger seat of his red, white and blue GMC van, barely pulled out of the parking lot when two Connecticut troopers in those Canadian Mounty-type hats and crisp green unis pulled him over in the driveway of Starbucks up the street.

Kari Stennis, a 23-year-old clerk with a platinum tongue stud who worked at Fry's Electronics, watched the arrest outside the window until police ordered her building evacuated.

Moments after she crossed the street, she heard a loud pop and upchucked on the spot, thinking the troopers shot and killed Salt Brumley.

But it was the sound of the exploding bomb—which wasn't potent enough to crack a single window in Starbucks.

Of course, Starbucks' windows are reinforced with a patented new synthetic to protect against terrorism.

The explosion was potent enough to make a hole the size of a cellphone in Brumley's chest and rain blood on the two crisp, proud pigs on their Harleys.

The sight of Seldon "Salt" Brumley's body slumped over the pavement haunted Kari Stennis for a long time.

Because of her tender stomach, Kari Stennis removed her tongue stud and fasted for four consecutive days.

Which, experts say, is the only sure-fire way to lose weight.

Especially if combined with moderate, daily exercise and compulsive calorie counting.

"I just couldn't believe this guy could have done something to bring out the feds," Kari Stennis said.

"We're not used to feds in little Rolla, Missouri."

She pronounced it "Mizzoura."

"Poor Salt—seeing him sitting that way in the gutter dead.

"He looked so average, so common, so confused."

**

Helmut Heydrich is a sleekly attractive 42-year-old white male, resembling a bit Conrad Veidt, the Forties Hollywood actor out of Germany who was typically cast as a sadistic Nazi officer.

Heydrich is also, by his own admission, a cannibal, who two-and-a-half years ago ate a microchip designer he had found through the Internet.

Heydrich's lawyer describes him as an "Aryan from the old school."

But when Helmut Heydrich strode into a courtroom in this central

German city of Rotenburg Wednesday morning, bearing erect, blond hair neatly buzzed, carrying an expensive leather briefcase and dressed in a gray pinstriped double-breasted suit, gray silk shirt, black and gray striped tie, and trendy mahogany Oxfords from Mephisto, he looked positively postmodern.

He looked, in truth, like yet another lawyer, a member of his legal defense team rather than a man accused of mutilating, sodomizing and consuming his houseguest.

The trial of Helmut Heydrich, 41, who airily confessed to a sex and cannibalism ritual with a willing victim who answered his Internet posting, has revolted and enthralled his fellow Germans since it began earlier this month.

Each of those categories: revulsion and enthrallment, has carved out a long and disheartening history in Germany.

The cannibalism, in March 2003, reads like an updated version of a dark fable from the Brothers Grimm, who transcribed their often morbid fairy stories in the nearby hamlet of Kassel, populating the richly forested countryside with dwarves, goblins, and at least one haggard, hemorrhoidal witch who loved to baste and roast children then savor them.

The German tabloids have been beside themselves with lurid details about the male they call the Cannibal of Rotenburg, after the secluded village where Heydrich lived with his tyrannical, bedridden mother in a ramshackle three-story wood house.

Where he trolled the Internet for Aryan males with a yen to be sodomized, slaughtered and eaten.

Were the desired males exclusively Aryan?

Evidently yes.

Beyond the gruesomely sexy details, all of which the obsessive-compulsive, techno-proficient Heydrich recorded with state-of-the-art video technology, the case raises thorny legal issues.

Hence an official German legal team recently spent a fortnight in the UK conferring with cannibalism experts in that once proud isle where even the most degraded sexual play has always been *comme il faut* among the bluebloods.

The primary issue from a legal standpoint is whether Heydrich can be found guilty of murder even though his victim, a 29-year-old male identified only as Bertolt B, a Bavarian, consented and even pleaded to be sodomized, mutilated and consumed.

The prosecution concedes that the victim was willing, but insists he was mentally unbalanced and moronic as well.

Does a moron know how to surf the Internet?

Undeniably.

The prosecution contends that Heydrich, a cellular phone programmer and admitted men's toilet gloryhole enthusiast, murdered his victim and ate him as a form of sexual gratification.

The prosecutor put it this way: "Herr Heydrich slaughtered his victim like a piece of livestock and treated him as an object of his fancy."

Arguably so; the point is that cannibalism itself is not a crime in Germany, meaning that particular legal avenue was closed to prosecutors.

Even after the depredations in the Nazi-era camps, cannibalism is not a crime in Germany?

Correct.

Gloryhole sex is a crime, of course, but only when there is proven deconstruction of property, such as a hole freshly drilled in the wall between two commodes.

"It is, you know, interestingly complicated," said Johann Herzfeld, director of the Institute for the Study of Criminology at Giessen University, "because here you have two Aryan males converging with the very same perverted fantasy, one approaching it from the, so to speak, obverse; the other from the reverse.

"One says, 'I want to sodomize, mutilate and consume you.'

"The other replies, 'I want to be sodomized, mutilated and consumed by you.'"

Heydrich's lawyer, the flamboyant US-trained Theo Adorno, contends that his client is guilty only of "cannibalizing on request," an illegal form of euthanasia in Deutschland that carries a maximum prison sentence of fourteen months.

Whereas a manslaughter conviction would put Heydrich in prison for up to 10 years.

Which means in effect that he would be relinquishing his ass for ten years?

If you're asking: would he be sodomized in prison? Yes, he would be. But probably for only five or six years, with good behavior. Moreover, institutional sodomy, forced or consensual, isn't the same plague here as it is in the US.

Given all the legal ambiguities, Professor Herzfeld said the case could end up in the Federal Constitutional Court.

The simplest way to keep Helmut Heydrich off the Internet, Herzfeld said, would be for the three distinguished judges to rule that he was suffering from "diminished responsibility" at the time of the killings and remand him to one of the "bunkers" (the informal name for the state-run psychiatric hospitals).

The trouble is a court-appointed forensic psychiatrist already vetted Heydrich and concluded that he was fit to stand trial.

Unless he reverses himself convincingly on the witness stand or severs and flambées his own penis, as he allegedly did to his victim, the judges would find it difficult to confine Heydrich to a mental institution.

"If the forensic psychiatrist concludes that he is responsible for his actions, there is no way to keep him away from the Internet for any length of time," said Wolfgang Schott, Professor of Psychiatry at the University of the Saarland.

The prospect of not putting Heydrich away seems to beguile the hundreds of German humans who have turned up at the nondescript courthouse here twice a week to take in the proceedings.

"If he were released he would pose a great danger to the public," said 64-year-old pensioner, Otto Stekl.

"This bloke and his mates were engaged in some very strange behavior.

"It could happen again, you know," Stekl said, grinning crookedly.

Heydrich offered a glimpse into his erotic netherworld in testimony on the first day of the trial.

Speaking softly in an even baritone, he said he posted advertisements on the Internet, under the pseudonym *Freek*, which said: "Honk your white BMW if you are a young Aryan male and want to be eaten."

He claimed to have gotten about 2,500 hits in the first three hours.

Four young Aryan males traveled to Rotenburg from different sectors of Germany to meet with Heydrich, were introduced to each other, and, according to his lawyer, Theo Adorno, engaged in "toilet sex" *en famille.*

When it became apparent that none of the four wanted the sex to cross the line into cannibalism, Heydrich permitted them to exit, according to Adorno.

The four Aryan males testified on Monday, not *en famille* but serially.

At their request the presiding judge closed the proceedings to the public, but some colorful testimony did leak into the media, including the odd fact that one of the four wasn't Aryan at all; he was Jewish, though uncircumcised.

With the fifth male, the true Aryan, Bertolt B, a cigar-smoking microchip designer and playwright from Munich, in Bavaria, Heydrich evidently found a human willing to go all the way.

As Heydrich ran a video camera, he spread his naked raunchy haunches on the plump, youngish cigar smoker's face; next he sodomized him with a large kitchen knife handle; then when the victim agreed to the removal of his penis, Heydrich severed the organ with the same knife, flambéed it and served it up for them to eat together.

They both partook of Bertolt B's severed, flambéed penis?

Allegedly.

Even as the victim was bleeding profusely?

Allegedly.

After the flambée, Heydrich used the same knife, along with a butcher's cleaver, to slash and chop Bertolt B to death, before hanging the carcass upside-down on a meat hook, carving it and ejaculating on it.

Heydrich claims to have kept the skull and flesh in plastic bags in his freezer.

Every now and again he defrosted a bag and ate the contents.

In all, he figured, he consumed about 49-and-a-half pounds of flesh.

"With every forkful of flesh I ate, I remembered Bertolt B," Heydrich said, according to Reuters.

"It was like taking Communion.

"I even smoked his cigars.

"Tasty Havanas from Cuba."

Heydrich told the court that his cannibalization of Bertolt B was the consummation of a dream he had had since his school days, when he fantasized about eating classmates.

Despite this, the court-appointed psychiatrist decided that while Heydrich "demonstrated a schizoid personality," he was not mentally ill, as such, and was thus fit to stand trial.

Heydrich's defense counsel, Theo Adorno, explained to the court that, unlike the factual circumstances of his cannibal client vis-à-vis Bertolt B, murder "must happen against somebody's will."

Whether or not his client is convicted of murder or manslaughter, Herr Adorno advised those planning similar forays into the world of cannibalism to "ensure both parties draw up a binding contract before the act takes place."

However, Bertolt B's lover, G. Lukacs, age 27, testified to the court that Bertolt B, with whom he said he enjoyed a normal sex life in Bavaria, never demonstrated the least desire to die or have his penis flambéed.

German experts say that while there may be hundreds, thousands, perhaps even tens of thousands of Germans with "cannibalistic tendencies," only a minuscule portion of those would be willing to see their fantasies through to their fatal conclusion as Bertolt B apparently did.

Internet messages which request humans for slaughter are often written off as jokes by other participants, most of whom stress that their interest in cannibalism is only a metaphor.

While Helmut Heydrich received thousands of responses to his postings, he is believed to have only met four other males besides Bertolt B—the three Aryans and fourth imaginary Aryan—none of whom proved willing to go through with the act.

And of the five males who physically transacted with Helmut Heydrich, only one, Bertolt B, from Munich, had purchased a one-way ticket to Rotenburg.

There are, however, fears that should the court punish Helmut Heydrich lightly in Friday's ruling, they will unwittingly encourage real cannibals to come out from behind their computers.

Quit the virtual, embrace the actual.

Yet if Heydrich is put away for life after Friday's ruling, Theo Adorno, his defense lawyer has argued, the true horror of murder, of which his client is not guilty, will be thereby diminished.

No wonder this trial has been riveting theater for courtroom regulars like the pensioner Otto Stekl, who said that most of the cases he attended involved burglaries, prostitution or drug busts.

For Stekl, the hard part is squaring the horror of Heydrich's story with his scrubbed, attractive appearance.

"He's sympathetic, you know. Very Aryan," Stekl said, adding with a nervous giggle, "he looks like the handsomest Aryan cannibal you could ever meet."

Verdict Delivered

A German court has convicted self-confessed cannibal Helmut Heydrich of manslaughter and sentenced him to eight years and six months in prison.

Heydrich, 42, admitted killing and eating Bertolt B after sado-masochistic sex, but insisted his victim had volunteered.

It has been Germany's most sensational trial since Nuremberg.

The verdict falls well short of the prosecution's demand for a 15-year sentence for sexual murder.

The defense counsel, Theo Adorno, had sought a verdict of illegal euthanasia, carrying a far shorter sentence of six months to five years, on the grounds that it had been "a form of mercy killing."

But while rejecting the defense's argument the court also ruled that Heydrich had had no "base motives" for the crime and settled on a manslaughter verdict.

Both were looking for the "ultimate jolt," Judge Volker Braun summarized to a packed courtroom.

"This was an act between two extremely disturbed people who each wanted something from the other."

Heydrich had not, the judge clarified, committed a murder in the legal sense, "but exhibited a behavior which is condemned in civilized society—namely the killing and butchering of a human being.

"Viewed legally, this is manslaughter, killing a person without being a murderer," he added.

Dressed in a navy blue double-breasted suit and maroon and pink striped tie, Heydrich sat impassively as the verdict was read out in court.

He has been in detention since the act occurred in 2003.

His lawyer, Theo Adorno, described him as a "model prisoner," and said he could be released on good behavior by 2008.

Prosecutors say they will appeal the verdict.

In his soft, even baritone, Heydrich informed the court that he plans to write his memoirs in order to persuade other people with similar fantasies to "restrain themselves."

Trader Joe's

We were sitting around the oak wood table drinking red wine and enumerating the virtues of Trader Joe's when there was a knock at the door.

Trader Joe's is popular in your circle?

Without question.

Late corporate capitalism, then, has not failed utterly?

Far from it.

[Pause]

You say there was a knock at the door...

Yes.
Come in, we called out.
Instead there was a pause, then three or four more knocks, louder.
Again one of us called out: Come in, the door is open.
Nothing.
I myself got up to look outside and nobody was there.
We looked at each other wonderingly, but let it pass and went back to our wine and conversation.

Went back to the enumeration of Trader Joe's virtues?

No.

The knocking at the door seemed to quash that.

I remember the story of the poet Coleridge being interrupted by the tailor from Porlock, I think it was, while he was composing "Kubla Khan."

After the tailor left, the poem took a very different turn.

Of course Coleridge was not drinking red wine.

He was ingesting laudanum of opium.

Lucky man.

Instead of opium and Absinthe, we have lite beer and blogs.

In any case, after the knocking at the door, the discussion turned to L.L. Bean.

Those honest Yankees from Freeport, Maine.

You must have ordered from them.

Never.

You order something from Bean in 1997, wear it a hundred times, then decide you don't like it and return it to them after the millennium.

They accept it without complaint.

Exchange it or refund your money.

Nobody at the oak wood table sipping red wine had a bad word to say about L.L. Bean.

How many of you were sitting at the oak wood table sipping red wine?

Not just number but gender distribution.

Five.

Two females, two males.

The fifth human's gender was ambiguous.

I imagine the ambiguous-gendered human would find it hard to order from L.L. Bean.

Not at all.
When s/he is feeling male she orders from the male catalog.
When s/he is feeling female she orders from the female catalog.
When s/he is feeling funky she orders from the fly fishing catalogue.

What sort of red wine were you drinking?

A Chilean Cabernet.
Full-bodied, on the dry side.
A serious Cab, but not heavy.
Bought for a very good price in Trader Joe's.

Pinochet's Chile.

Neruda's Chile is how we view it.
Pinochet was the fascist genocider, right?
Isn't he dead?
If he's not dead he's ancient.
Once you pass a certain age you might as well be dead.
And the age keeps getting younger.
Especially in the US of course.

Pinochet's in exile.
Spain, I believe.
Or it could be that Spain deported him back to Chile.

[Pause]

So we were sitting around the oak wood table praising L.L. Bean
and sipping our Chilean red when there was another knock at the door,

louder than before, three loud raps.

Again we called out: Come in, the door's open.

Silence.

I went to the door a second time, opened it, looked outside.

Nobody there.

The wind?

No, it was a calm night.

The moon was full and bright.

It was a blessing to be alive and middle class under the banner of freedom.

Again we exchanged a look, sipped our Chilean Cab and resumed talking.

About L.L. Bean?

No.

The knocking at the door seemed to quash the Bean dialogue.

Was it a dialogue or an enumeration of their virtues?

Both, as I recall.

Nobody at the table had any idea who was knocking at the door?

No.

The humans in our circle either contact us on their cellphones or email.

In a pinch they'll fax.

Showing up in the middle of the night and rapping at the door is not particularly cool.

Unless of course it's an emergency.

You keep the outside door unlocked?

I live in a gated community.
Surveillance 24/7.
It's written in the mission statement.
I thought I'd mentioned that.

Electronic surveillance or human?

Electronic.
Human surveillance has gone the way of the public phone.

What time was it?

Ten-thirty-five p.m. on a Thursday in May.

Work the next a.m.

Not for me.
I sleep in on Fridays.
Do a bit of work in the afternoon.
Electronically.
We refilled our glasses...

With the same Chilean Cabernet?

Absolutely.
Trader Joe's agents scour the globe to buy products in great quantities.
That's how they charge a good price.
The conversation turned to Home Depot.
You've heard people say about a certain place: You can get everything but the kitchen sink.

Well at Home Depot you can get everything *plus* the kitchen sink.
And always at a competitive price.
You've shopped in Home Depot, right?

No.
I'm not a home owner.
I sleep where I can.
Everything I need I carry in this cloth bag.

Impressive.
I guess you don't ski; you'd have to be Houdini to fit skis into that cloth bag.
By the way, you don't have to be a home owner to enjoy Home Depot.
Robert Venturi, the architect, wrote provocatively of the Las Vegas "esthetic."
Venturi made a virtue of ruthless, slapdash capitalism.
You must have heard of Venturi.
Well, there's a Home Depot esthetic.

Very male, no?

Home Depot?
Male?
Yes and no.
It smells of wood chips, machine oil and honest sweat.
Tattoos everywhere.
On the bodies, though, of men *and* women.
Post-postmodern females shop in Home Depot.
These females tend not to follow the conventional strictures.

[Pause]

Was that the end of the knocks at the door?

No, there was a loud series of raps while we were enumerating the virtues of Home Depot.

This time the ambiguously gendered person got up to open the door...

And?

There was a young woman, slender, dark-complected, in a veil, or hijab—
Is that what it's called?
Hijab?

I believe so.

Well, above the veil—or hijab—we could see her sad, dark eyes.
She was holding an infant to her breast.

You could see her sad, dark eyes and the infant at her breast from where you sat?

Yes.

What did she want?

Haven't a clue.
What *could* she want at that time of night?
In that neighborhood?
Alms, probably.
We didn't let her in.

[Pause]

Trader Joe's

So the electronic surveillance failed you after all?

What's that?

Your electronic surveillance failed you.

I suppose so, yes.
Why are you grinning?
Even technology is fallible, is that it?
And for some obscure reason you find that laughable.

Terror Couture

File

A brace of white smug ramrod-straight Marine recruiters in their parade unis, ribbons and medals on their stuck-out chests, descend into the mean streets where they've never been in real time. Harlem, Compton, Oakland, Milwaukee, Newark, Watts, Philly, Detroit City…

"Yo kid, how old are you? 17? You look older. You're a big kid. You still in school? You dropped out to work to help your family. What kind of work? Bagging groceries. Well, that sucks. How would you like to make a whole lot more bread than you're making and be a proud Marine at the same time? Marine Corps, travel, girls, money… You ain't sure. You like rap, right? Did you know that Big Diddy Mo-Fukk was a Marine? That's right. Three of his posse joined up with him. Cool, right? You're a big strong kid. How cool do you think you'd look in this uni? Here, let me give you my card. How about you give me your cell phone number—I know all you dudes carry cells— and I'll call you tonight at 7:00. You available at 7:00? Cool. 'Cause I'd like to see you at the Marine Corps recruiting booth on Monday at 8:30? Too early? We'll let's make it 9:30. You know where it's at, right? Steve Biko Street, across from the multiplex. What's your name, by the way? Karim. Cool, Karim, I'll phone you tonight at 7:00 to remind you. And, man, I'm looking forward to seeing you in that Marine Corps uni."

Back in the day a standing president waging a stubborn war would reinstate the draft, stockpile working-class cannon fodder. But a draft now would alienate the white middle class, so it's shanghaiing one Karim at a time.

Format

After eight weeks of basic, Karim and all the Karims are inoculated and shipped to Iraq where they kill, are killed, get sick or wounded, languish in the desert. If alive, they finally return home after eighteen months with trauma, loss of limbs, Gulf War Syndrome, or all of the above, having been subjected to depleted uranium and significantly reduced veteran's benefits.

With more than 500 million tons of radioactive depleted uranium (DU) stored in various states of nuclear decay at government repositories throughout the country, the Pentagon encourages weapons industries to use DU in their tank rounds, helicopter gunship rounds, artillery, bombs, and Cruise missiles because of its penetrating power, blasting into rock or bunker, ferreting out Osama bin Laden or that other geek from his spider hole.

Best of all, the DU is free. An expedient way of removing nuclear waste, with its half life of nearly 5 billion years, out of mainstream America. Hell, it's a lot cheaper than bribing American Indians to bury it on their rez.

An impartial onsite investigation in Iraq after the post-9/11 invasion found that, "40 percent of the initial mass of the DU penetrators was converted to radioactive oxide while 60 percent was left on and around the impact area in solid form. Contamination included uranium oxides, unstable unexploded ordnance and byproducts of exploded ordnance [all of which] pose a grave risk through inhalation, ingestion or wound contamination." **

When the DU-laced ordnance is produced, the Pentagon purchases it, thereby achieving three worthy objectives: ridding the US of more DU; making the weapons industrialists richer than they are; and, after the examples of Hiroshima/Nagasaki, wreaking apocalyptic damage on the enemy, the enemy's children, grandchildren, great-grandchildren...

View

The war is over, the good guys won in a rout, one of the top five fastest military victories on record, according to FOX TV.

Except the war ain't over.

Thanks to insurgent terrorists with their rocks and stones and suicide bombings.

What you have is tribal warfare of the sort that Arabs and their desert cousins have been waging since the Tower of Babel.

Sunni vs. Shia; Kurd vs. Iraqi; Turk vs. Kurd; Bedouin vs. camels. Whatever.

Beheadings. Mindless chaos.

The US is doing what it can to reconstruct vital infrastructures, after having destroyed those same vital infrastructures, in the process of insuring the peace.

American fatalities? You can count them on the fingers of your hands. And feet.

Altogether the occupation goes swimmingly.

Well, there've been a few blips.

The torture thing at Abu Ghraib—handful of homesick reservists maybe pushing it a little too far.

That issue's been addressed.

The puppet government waits in the wings.

The only problem is they're Arabs.

But they know where their paycheck comes from.

In any case, the coalition forces will maintain a modest presence in Iraq, 175,000 or so, in and around the oil refineries and other vital centers.

File

Super sexy models in "extreme" military gear strut down a fashion runway while high tech warplanes in furious flight flash across the walls.

Thus begins pop icon Madonna's video "American Life," composed after 9/11 but before the invasion of Iraq.

Madonna sings and vamps against a black backdrop while giant videogame fireballs erupt over her shoulders.

Hysterical generic Arabs mass and gesticulate in the streets.

The video's climax features Madonna and a dozen bulky females in camo crashing a Humvee through the backdrop, then strutting ominously about the stage, tugging at their crotches while spraying water cannon at the cheering crowd.

Those shots are interfaced with rapid edits of American postmodern bombers dropping bombs, generating massive explosions.

Format

Madonna claims she wanted the video to express dramatically her virtuous sentiments about war, materialism, and the haute-couture industry.

In the meantime the war had begun, the white hats had achieved a sparkling Blitzkrieg triumph with virtually no losses of lives on the US side.

American pride and xenophobia were at an unprecedented high.

Given the emotional climate of the US, Madonna decided to edit the footage to make it less controversial.

But then she, or her handlers, were still nervous, so she withdrew the video altogether.

Those media outlets that possessed the unedited Madonna video had themselves an expensive mistake they would be able to cash in on big time in due course.

View

Louise Ciccone (aka Madonna) called a press conference:

"Due to the violent and unpredictable state of the world and out of the utmost respect for the armed forces, who I whole-heartedly support and pray for, I do not want offend anyone who might misinterpret the meaning of this video, which is why I withdrew it."

I won't pass gas on her born-again patriotism and sudden penchant for prayer, but Madonna, who's a middle-aged mom as we all know, looked smashing at her news conference in a black silk, body-clinging jumpsuit (no bra) with gold and green digitized camo accenting, trousers tucked into calf-high desert combat boots. Strategic strands of dyed blond hair peeked out from under an army black beret, and a pair of gold-plated handcuffs dangled provocatively from her left—Yes, I said left!—hip.

File

The stars and stripes were everywhere: on basketball jerseys and shorts, on the Nike brand sneakers, on the glass backboards, and (about the length and width of a B-17 bomber) on the ceiling of the Pepsi Center where the Denver Nuggets play their home games.

Post-9/11, game night, Nuggets vs. Atlanta Hawks.

Instead of singing the National Anthem once before the contest, the National Anthem was now sung at the start and God Bless America at the resumption of the second half, accompanied each time by a contingent of flag-carrying honor guard representing the four armed services: Army, Navy, Air Force, Marine Corps.

Instead of standing more or less quietly, shuffling in anticipation of the game, the players were instructed to stand absolutely still and place their right hand, palm down, on the stars and stripes decal in the area of their heart.

Saad Amir Mohammed refused to comply. The second-year, high-scoring shooting guard for the Nuggets had pasted a black cross on his left chest where the flag decal was, and when the National Anthem came on he turned his back to the honor guard, keeping his hands at his sides.

Born Floyd Washington in Natchez, Mississippi, Saad Amir Mohammed was first-string all-American at LSU and the third leading scorer in the nation. He entered the pros after his sophomore year, drafted number four in the first round by the Denver Nuggets.

Format

Saad Amir Mohammed started the game against the Hawks but was pulled after two minutes and didn't play again that night.

The next day the NBA commissioner suspended him for 20 games without any provision for a hearing. The commissioner also ordered the player to explain his actions.

The players' union, meanwhile, protested feebly that 20 games was a very long time for any infraction, especially during the last half of the season in the chase for the division title. At the same time, the union criticized Mohammed for his "insensitivity and lack of patriotism."

Saad Amir Mohammed refused to call a press conference, but he did release this statement to the league and pertinent media outlets:

"My name is Saad Amir Mohammed and my foremost duty is to God. I have thought about this for a long time and still can only see it this way: It is wrong to make war on the poor people of Iraq, to bomb them and to cause them great suffering. And to kill and torture them in the name of the Christian or Jewish God, as is being done, is doubly wrong.

"The attacks on 9/11 were a bad thing and I am very sorry that innocent people died, but that is still not justification for this country to behave like a wounded giant that blindly strikes back, as it did in its full-scale attack on Afghanistan and, especially, on Iraq. I say 'especially on Iraq' because there is no evidence at all that they had anything to do with 9/11.

"All I can say now is that I acted according to my beliefs, with the counsel of my God and my family. My career as a basketball player who makes a lot of money, what the NBA establishment, the media and other people think of me—none of that can matter in the face of this terrible tragedy of unprovoked, full-scale war on a very poor country.

"Allahu akbar!"

View

That was the last game Saad Amir Mohammed played in the NBA. He was waived two weeks later. No other team claimed him. The Denver Nuggets sued to legally refrain from paying his multi-million dollar salary under the "extraordinary circumstances" and won the suit.

Mohammed dropped out of sight for nearly eight months, but then resurfaced in dramatic fashion. He was identified by two witnesses as the trigger man in a failed gas station robbery and murder of a police officer outside Baton Rouge, Louisiana.

The crucial evidence was a Denver Nuggets home jersey with Mohammed's name, number, and blacked-out American flag decal found at the scene. What was the jersey doing there? Nobody professed to know; the fact that it was there was unassailable.

Saad Amir Mohammed, who denied any participation in the murder and claimed he was set up, is now waiting to be executed by lethal injection on death row in Angola State Prison.

File

A Caucasian male wearing a false long beard and black Muslim-style jubbah with *Osama bin Laden* stenciled in gold on the back crashed Prince William's 21st birthday party at Windsor Castle last month.

The intruder who somehow managed to elude officers of the Royal Protection Service bounded onto the stage, where he raised his sheet-like garment, exposing his naked buttocks to the distinguished guests.

Then he lunged for the slender, passive prince, kissing him on both pale cheeks before being apprehended.

The intruder, evidently in his thirties, was reportedly a dropout from Sandhurst Military Academy. He refused to supply even the most basic information, identifying himself only as Terror Couture, obviously not his real name.

Since the intrusion the commander of palace security has been removed, and nine members of his retinue have been either demoted or transferred to duties in the UK's remotest former colonies. Those, that is, which have not been fractured by post-colonial civil war and terrorism.

The intruder himself, "Terror Couture," will "most certainly be charged," according to Scotland Yard.

Format

UK and US government investigators working in tandem have uncovered further information about the intruder who calls himself Terror Couture. He is 37-years-old, a drop-out *not* from elite Sandhurst, as initially reported, but from a technical college called Muggeridge in east London. He was not born in the UK but in County Cork, Ireland. He is Roman Catholic and reportedly has several times expressed his affinity with Sinn Fein, the revolutionary arm of the IRA.

Moreover, according to the CIA, Terror Couture is a devotee of Theodore Kaczynski, the infamous American "Unabomber" and diagnosed schizophrenic. Kaczynski's revolutionary screed, The *Unabomber Manifesto*, was found in Terror Couture's messy bedsitter in the rundown Earl's Court section of London.

Kaczynski claimed he was (actually *is*; he's alive but sedated and securely institutionalized) a female trapped inside a male's body. When his plea for a sex-change operation was denied, he went on his murderous rampage of bombing innocent technicians of the sacred.

It could be then that Terror Couture's obscene buttocks display to the royal audience and groping of Prince William were a nod, or even an *hommage*, to his declared idol, Kaczynski, the Unabomber.

More significant is Terror Couture's choice of disguise; dressing up as Osama bin Laden only months after 9/11 is scarcely a joking matter. But was Terror Couture merely dressing up, or was there, as has been reported, a firmer link between him and Al-Qaeda or even Osama bin Laden himself?

View

The UK, under pressure from its firmer cousin across the Atlantic, has extradited Terror Couture to the US, where he will be tried or held without trial, depending on whether his reported links to Al-Qaeda are validated.

If the CIA confirms Terror Couture's connection to Al-Qaeda he will officially be labeled an unlawful combatant and in all likelihood be transferred to the terrorist stockade in Guantánamo Bay where he will be "interrogated."

What has Terror Couture to say for himself?

"So sorry you took this the wrong way.

"My intention was to make people laugh not fart.

"My intention was comedy not politics.

"My mentor is Benny Hill not Joan of Arc.

"Go ahead and torture me.

"The blood you draw will be my fool's cap.

"We laughers will still end up burying you murderers."

Salaam

When the Palestinian terrorist opened his shirt to display the explosives taped to his chest, the Israeli shop owner pointed to a large cast iron pot simmering on the stove. It contained cabbage, potatoes, green onions, and—unmistakably—a tiny human hand.

**

When the Palestinian opened his shirt to display the explosives taped to his chest, the Israeli shop owner on the crowded Jerusalem street pointed to the old pot simmering on the stove. Cabbage, potatoes, green onions, and a tiny human hand.

The Palestinian was young, slender, with black eyes and the tracings of a black mustache.

The shop owner was wiry with bloodshot eyes and a once black now grey and white mustache.

They glared into each other's eyes.

Then, as the young Palestinian raised his fist, the old man raised his arm with numbers tattooed on it.

The young man pronounced the word *Palestine* even as the old man uttered the word *Auschwitz*.

Each in his own tongue.

**

When the Palestinian opened his shirt to display the explosives taped to his chest the Israeli shop owner pointed to the large pot simmering on the stove. It contained cabbage, potatoes, green onions, and—conspicuously—a tiny human hand.

Palestinian, —I know that hand. It is my sister's hand.

Israeli, —You are wrong. It is my sister's hand.

—The hand is tiny. You are an old man.

—I was young then as you. In another country.

**

Israeli, —So you are a suicide bomber.

—Freedom fighter.

—Murdering hundreds of anonymous Jews will provide this freedom?

—It is the only way left.

—You have heard of the word genocide?

—Every day of my life I hear this word.

**

When the Palestinian opened his shirt displaying the explosives taped to his chest the Israeli shop owner on the crowded Jerusalem street pointed to the large pot simmering on the stove. Cabbage, potatoes, green onions, and a tiny human hand.

Glaring into each other's eyes.

Israeli, —What is it that you want?

—The Jews to give us back our land. That we can live in peace.

—And if I tell you that this land in Jerusalem and beyond is not yours but ours. Historically ours.

—Let the United Nations decide.

—And the Jew-haters in the UN. What about them?

**

Israeli, —You are prepared to murder yourself and hundreds of ordinary people you do not know who happen to be Jews. Why? Because of a principle?

—If this principle means truth, then yes, God willing, I am prepared to join my martyred freedom-fighting brothers and sisters.

—There are many others who feel as you do?

—I cannot give numbers. But I have never met a Palestinian who was not prepared to die for freedom.

—And if you did meet one?

—I would refuse to shake his hand.

**

When the Palestinian opened his shirt and displayed the explosives taped to his chest the Israeli shop owner pointed to the large pot simmering on the stove. It contained cabbage, potatoes, green onions, and—unmistakably—a tiny human hand.

—You Jews are cannibals.

—The opposite is true. We have been cannibalized.

—You are talking about Nazis. You cannot stop talking about your Nazis.

—No.

—That is the problem with you Jews. You live in the past.

—No. We live in the present under the weight of the past. There is no other way.

**

Palestinian, —These Nazis that so obsess you. You have become them.

—What are you saying?

—Just that. You Israelis in your crisp uniforms with your advanced weapons slaughter us and degrade us as the Nazis did you.

—What you are parroting here I have heard before. It has become fashionable. It is an unspeakable slander. And coming from you with genocide taped and strapped across your body!

**

When the Palestinian freedom fighter opened her blouse to display the explosives taped to her body the Israeli shop owner's daughter gestured to her breast then pointed to the Palestinian's breast.

They gazed long into each other's dark eyes.

Then the Palestinian jerked her head to the side, reached under her blouse, detonated.

That is one version. The other version follows.

After looking long at each other, the Palestinian freedom fighter nodded her head once, slowly.

Carefully, she disarmed the explosives.

Then she and the shop owner's daughter embraced and arm in arm stepped out into the turbulent Jerusalem street.

Mustache

What do Adolph Hitler, Joseph Stalin and Saddam Hussein have in common?

The answer, according to a just-released—but already controversial—study, is a "fastidiously tended black mustache."

Each of the three brutal despots wore a black mustache that was his pride and joy.

Each possessed a *valet de chambre*, an adolescent or teenage boy, who preened and manicured and fussed over his master's mustache.

The boy, alternatively communicating in Deutsch, Russian or Arabic, accompanied his master everywhere while transporting a customized manicure set, magnifying hand-mirror, curling iron, beeswax, and masculine-scented toilet water, such that the savage dictator would pause even in the midst of a bloody incursion to have his black mustache addressed.

The question of course is why?

Why—when there are dissidents to torture, civil liberties to suppress and sovereign countries to invade—pay inordinate attention to a mustache?

The short answer is "malignant narcissism."

That is the diagnosis which a distinguished team of psychologists led by Dr. F. Lennard Hunt of Georgetown University, in Washington DC, and Dr. Moses Herzog of the University of Haifa, in Israel, has put forth.

The psychological profile (referred to informally as the "mustache study") of three of the most infamous tyrants in history was jointly commissioned by the US Air Force "Counterproliferation Center" and by the Central Intelligence Agency's "Political Accountability" file.

It has stirred controversy in and out of the government: from the left because it "coarsens in simplistic ways" the dictators' psychology; from the right because its "trivializes and in effect whitewashes" the dictators' crimes.

According to Drs Hunt and Herzog, malignant narcissism is defined as "overweening ambition, excessive egomania, hypersensitivity to perceived slights, incapacity to experience empathy, compulsive genocidal ideation, and an extreme narcissistic attention to the cultivation and elaboration of the black mustache."

Malignant narcissism is now officially included in the *Diagnostic and Statistical Manual of Mental Disorders* (*DSM*), published by the American Psychiatric Association.

The *DSM*'s current edition is 1,270 pages long and contains 378 disorders.

It can be ordered via any legitimate bookseller, or discounted through the APA's official website: www.supine.com.

The mustache study makes the crucial point that "bad does not necessarily equal mad."

That is, malignant narcissism does not automatically signify psychosis.

Indeed, the malignant narcissist is often disarmingly charming and expert at persuasion and manipulation even without the threat of punishment.

In Drs. Hunt and Herzog's words: "The supreme leader's overabundant narcissism is expressed in grandiosity, supreme self-confidence, and the smooth assurance that he possesses precisely what the world needs.

"For many ignorant, oppressed third-world humans of color, those attributes add up to an irresistible combination."

Even counterterrorism experts sympathetic in principle to the study, concede that psychoanalyzing political despots, especially retroactively, after they've been long dead, is a "dicey business."

And the psychologists responsible for the study are quick to caution that, absent objective data and/or verifiable anecdotal records, any psychological profile must be provisional.

At the same time, Drs Hunt and Herzog maintain that, "malignant narcissism [is as] close to hitting the nail on the head," as possible, and a poll of psychologists and psychiatrists from first world countries around the globe would seem to concur.

As far as the dead Hitler and Stalin are concerned, the proof of malignant narcissism is in the pudding.

Nazi crematoria, Soviet gulags;

The fearsomely sexy Gestapo, the brutal Purges;

Hitler's vegetarianism, Stalin's Siberia;

Aryan fetishism, vodka mania…

With tyrannical Saddam Hussein, who, despite the US's earnest efforts to "decapitate" him, is, with his coal-black mustache, evidently still alive and devising chemical and biological weapons of mass destruction (WMD), the profile is on firmer ground, thanks to the US coalition's shock and awe campaign to liberate Iraq.*

While the liberation was proceeding, Iraqis, reportedly fueled by hashish, looted their own museums which contained invaluable artifacts dating back to ancient Mesopotamia.

Enemies of the US have asserted that American liberators deliberately left the museums unguarded, thus encouraging the Iraqis to loot and pillage.

But why employ even a single one of the US's essential 1,800 tanks, 490 helicopter gunships, 2,600 armored vehicles, and countless missiles to protect a museum filled with charred bones, shattered urns and scraps of tile?

The inescapable fact is that no sooner are the subjects released from the manacles of fanatical Islam than they revert to their violently anarchistic primal state.

To effect the US-led liberation with a minimum of casualties, depleted uranium in the invading army's bombs, tank and artillery rounds poisoned the southern city of Basra in Desert Storm during the previous incursion in 1991, orchestrated by Bush *père*, leaving an estimated 48 percent of children in that city fatally ill with cancer.

In 2003, Bush the younger, using something like 100 times more depleted uranium than in 1991, repoisoned Basra, Baghdad, and other strategic cities, towns and hamlets throughout the benighted country.

This time, the US assured France, Germany, Japan, and other oil-poor bleeding hearts that the deaths from cancer will be fewer, because the current Bush has lifted the embargo on vital hospital equipment and will soon be "sky-dropping" emergency medical supplies to win the hearts and minds of the Iraqi people.

The sky-dropped supplies will include Coca Cola, Microsoft hardware and Prozac, but will not include barbiturates, morphine or other drugs which have the capacity to alleviate pain while inducing euphoria.

As part of the US-led liberation, Saddam Hussein's seven palaces were breached uncovering an opulence worthy of *Arabian Nights*.

It featured bejeweled, perfumed inner sanctums laden with porno-graphic wall hangings, from which Saddam, reclining on outsized pillows while having his boy tend to his mustache, viewed unspeakable tortures through one-way mirrors.

Those tortured were his enemies: Shias, Kurds, apostate Sunnis...

To say that their genitals were excised by their own wives, mothers or children, and fed to starved hyenas is merely to cite one of the less outlandish punishments.

Directly beneath the opulence of his palaces with their inlaid jewels, exotic marble, and Kamasutra debauchery were reinforced concrete and lead bunkers fitted with munitions (purchased from France and China) and virulent chemical and biological agents.

"There, telescoped, is Saddam Hussein's psychology," Drs Hunt and Herzog assert.

"A grandiose façade but underneath it a fully elaborated siege state, prepared in paranoid fashion for betrayal, assault, or, more usually, a pre-emptive first strike."

The psychological study attributes the Iraqi despot's genocidal mega-lomania to his early childhood.

While pregnant with Saddam, his mother, highly strung to begin with, suffered the deaths of her husband, sister, elder son, and pet ocelot; as a result of which she tried to rip the fetal pre-born Saddam from her teeming womb, thus committing suicide.

However, she was "forcibly prevented by a good Samaritan rabbi who, in effect, became Saddam's benefactor."

Since his birth Saddam Hussein, far from cherishing his "benefactor," has in fact despised all Jews in a reaction that Drs Hunt and Herzog have labeled "malignant narcissistic denial" of the unacceptable circumstances of his own conception.

Via the same psychotic reasoning, because the Samaritan rabbi was bearded, Saddam Hussein has chosen to wear a black mustache rather than the long beard and whiskers that Islamic despots customarily affect.

If you wonder how at Saddam's age his mustache is still coal black, ask one of his adolescent valets.

*"**One** of his adolescent valets?" How many does he have?*

You mean "had." How many? A few dozen. Half of them were officially castrated. Castrati, eunuchs, geldings, capons. Others were hermaphrodites. Two sexes in one. If you interpret this as suggesting that Mr. Saddam Sodom was an utterly debauched switch-hitter, that's your privilege.

Drs Hunt and Herzog emphasize that, though it might seem otherwise, malignant narcissism is not an exclusively Arab or even Islamic trait.

Nor is malignant narcissism limited to genocidal despots with oily pores and fastidiously cultivated black mustaches.

"In a civilized country, in a less problematic time, with a different set of coordinates, Saddam Hussein could have become a corporate executive or a crusading dentist or even a millionaire attorney in suspenders, with his thinning hair in a pony tail.

"His ambition, paranoia and extreme, indiscriminate cruelty might then have been modulated by legal codes and refined by the civilized mores of a free society."

Which civilized mores of which free society are you signifiying? Not France?

No. Too self-righteous and finicky.

Not the UK?

No. They don't even have the stones to wipe their arse without big American bro in the damn loo egging them on.

Not the new old Germany?

Nein, motherfucker.

Not the shifting tundra of Russia?

Hell, they're in the throes of a collective post-Communist psychosis.

I have this queasy feeling. You're talking about old gloryhole, the indomitable Stars and Stripes, aren't you?

You have a problem with that?

No, huh-uh, I don't have a problem.

*Update: Saddam Hussein has been captured, flushed out of his "spider hole." He now wears a trimmed pepper and salt beard.

Mustache

**

A French woman who alleged she had been the subject of an anti-Semitic attack invented the story, police sources now say.

The alleged admission came shortly after she was taken into custody, four days after the alleged assault on a commuter train in the suburbs north of Paris.

The 24-year-old woman claimed six men accused her of being Jewish, then forcibly cut off her clothes with sharp, long knives and spray-painted swastikas on her body, front and back.

The woman, who is not Jewish, has been detained for falsely reporting a crime, state prosecutor Didier Merleau-Ponty told AFP news agency.

She could face up to six months in prison and an 8,000 euro ($10,000) fine if convicted.

The case has sparked widespread condemnation amid concerns that racist and anti-Semitic attacks are on the rise in France, which of course has a long and sordid history of such uprisings.

The men, described as of North African appearance and indeterminate age, are also said to have deliberately upended the woman's 8-month-old infant from its stroller.

The child fell on its head but was reportedly uninjured.

The woman claimed that about 20 people witnessed the attack but that nobody offered her support.

However, investigators, studying footage from surveillance cameras at the train station where the six alleged North African attackers were supposed to have exited, found no evidence to support the woman's claim.

Nor has a single witness come forth even after urgent appeals in the newspapers and on television.

Now police sources who requested anonymity say that under "firm questioning" the woman has recanted her accusations. She has admitted cutting off her own clothes and spray-painting the swastikas on her naked body with the help of her boyfriend who is also in custody. Presumably she spray-painted the front of her body and her boyfriend spray-painted the back. Like her, the boyfriend is neither Jewish nor North African, but French and white.

Le Monde, the left-leaning French daily, reports that the young woman had filed several complaints in the past about being the victim of racist or fascist violence.

The reported brutality of the attack on the woman, its anti-Semitic character and the fact that no one came to her help provoked outrage. It also added to the growing concern over racist and anti-Semitic attacks.

President Jacques Chirac, who condemned the alleged assault as "pitiless and reprehensible," said he would deny clemency to any prisoner serving a sentence for a racist or anti-Semitic crime.

Government spokesman Jean-Francois Irigaray told RTL radio that the rising trend of anti-Semitic attacks was "a genuine evil" in France, even if the woman's case "proved to be imagined rather than real, as such."

Human Shield

Me, I go six-five, 269.

Which is three, maybe three-and-a-half pounds more than when I was playing football.

I played tight end for the USC Trojans and was a consensus All-America in my senior year.

But when the Washington Redskins drafted me in the high first round they turned me into a middle linebacker.

In their scheme that meant a lot of freelancing which was the way I liked it.

The Redskins prided themselves on their special teams and I was a big part of that too.

I ran the 40 in 4.5 so that I worked up a full head of steam when I made a hit.

And that was without anabolic steroids or other illegal power compounds.

You name it, I swallowed it. I swallowed or injected anything I could get away with.

My teammates called me Hit Man.

I won't lie, I liked the contact.

The problem was I kept getting concussions.

After the thirteenth concussion I experienced memory loss and occasional blackouts.

This was halfway through my fourth year in the league and I was having a pro-bowl season.

My linebacker coach said: Memory loss has nothing to do with making a killer hit.

We were vying for the playoffs and Coach wanted me to finish the season.

But I took the doc's advice and hung 'em up for good.

I retired from football and got into law enforcement.

At the federal level.

Law enforcement always appealed to me.

I was looking for another way besides football to be very violent legally.

Even before I had a chance to send out feelers the Secretary contacted me.

Not the Secretary himself, of course, one of his staff.

The staff guy said the Secretary was a big-time fan of the Washington Redskins and heard me say at my press conference that with my football days behind me I wanted to get into law enforcement.

He said the Secretary admired the smash-mouth morality inculcated by the National Football League.

He said that back in the day the Secretary played JV football for a year at Princeton.

Second-string quarterback, I think it was.

Maybe it was third-string.

He said the Secretary was looking for a few good men to protect him, his family, his office, his personal golf course, and the honor of our nation.

Did I wish to apply for the position?

Hell yeah.

I was called in and four staff people shot questions at me.

Was I a patriot? Was I a good Christian? Would I give up my life for my country? Did I do drugs?

I answered them three strong yeses and a no.

Was I a fornicator? Did I have emotional ups and downs? Would I describe myself as a compassionate conservative?

I answered them two strong no's and a yes.

Next I was administered four separate drug tests ten days apart and passed them all with flying colors.

They offered me the job.

Needless to say, it was for a lot less money than I made playing football.

But unlike some other professional athletes I was not a high liver with gold-plated teeth, diamond earrings, a posse, illegitimate kids, and a different car toy for every finger and toe.

If the preceding sounds like a coded reference to African-American athletes, that's your problem.

I actually managed to save a lot of what I earned.

I still hadn't met the Secretary in the flesh.

It was explained to me that he was very busy with the war and terrorism and the homeland security act.

With presiding over his family and his church work.

With rescinding life sentences in federal cases and imposing the death penalty.

As a matter of principle, the Secretary was devoted to capital punishment and wanted it implemented without exception.

If the defendant is prepared to plea-bargain, if the defendant is retarded or mentally ill, if the defendant has "reasonable cause" to protest his innocence.

None of that matters one little bit.

Reject the liberal hand wringing, execute the defendant and do it in a timely manner.

Meanwhile, in cities throughout the country, especially in DC, the radical protests were spinning out of control.

Ignorant people, young and old, sympathized with the enemy, were misinformed, or simply had no faith in our government and our democratic institutions.

I was the one that killed that radical protester.

Did I mean to kill him?

Not really.

I didn't approve of what he was doing.

I hated what he was doing.

But it's not my place to be his judge and executioner.

My charge was to protect the Secretary whatever it took.

It could be the radical protester did not intend to physically harm the Secretary.

I was not in position to read his mind.

Everything was moving too fast for that.

My job is to react.

What I saw was three radical protesters in black hooded sweatshirts break through the cordon and make a beeline for the motorcade.

That's a no-no, zero tolerance, end of discussion.

Therefore me and my partner Del, who never played pro ball but was an all-conference middle linebacker for the Alabama Crimson Tide.

Del and I—we cut off the three radical protesters and, boom!, took them out.

Del is 6-4, 268, six percent body fat.

Ran the 40 in 4.6 before he blew out both knees.

Del whacked the first two and I popped the third.

I hit him with both forearms in the chest.

What I'm saying is I made a point of not hitting him high, in the head and face area.

I saw that he was a skinny radical protester and I pulled back a little bit.

I guess I whacked him hard enough to kill him.

Some of the law enforcement folks claim he was on drugs and more vulnerable to a hit.

The ACLU and so on—they deny it.

The official autopsy report said that crack cocaine and methamphetamine were found in his system

The ACLU and so on say the autopsy was rigged.

I'm twenty-nine now and I've played the game of football since I was four-and-a-half.

I think I can tell the difference between a hard and a not-so-hard hit.

I thumped that radical protester moderate, not hard.

Now they're saying — the ACLU and so on — that he had a weak heart. Uh-huh.

He should've had **Weak-Hearted Radical Protester** stenciled in yellow on his black hooded sweatshirt.

My orders were clear-cut: If any unauthorized human *or subhuman* moves toward the Secretary, stop him in his tracks, period.

If the radical protester gets by me, I splatter him with my Walther P99 sidearm.

But there's no way in hell he gets by me.

Same deal with Del.

The ACLU and so on — what they really want to do is lynch me.

Flaming liberals, they have a long-time vendetta against lawful murder and professional sports.

Why not make an example of me.

Except it ain't gonna happen.

The Secretary's office did some homework on the dead radical protester.

The name he went by was Rex Eagle.

Born in Hayward, California.

Twenty-four years old.

In and out of jail since he was sixteen.

Drug possession, gang-banging, tagging, loitering…

In jail was where he turned into a Maoist terrorist.

Pledged to overthrow the US by any means possible.

Which is the name of his organization: By Any Means Possible.

With terrorist cells in Yemen, Libya, the Sudan, Baghdad, North Korea, Pakestine.

This same Rex Eagle trained in Afghanistan with Al-Qaeda operatives and in the Gaza Strip with Arafat.

Was he a Muslim? Did he speak Arab? Did he pray to Allah?

That I can't tell you.

Whatever training Rex Eagle got, it must not've been physical.

Skinny radical punk that couldn't take a hit.

The Secretary commended me and Del for zapping the radical protesters.

Not personally, of course.

In an e-mail sent by a staff person on the Secretary's behalf.

The Secretary told me not to worry.

Rex Eagle was a proven terrorist and premature mass murderer of American patriots.

The other side had no case.

Didn't have a pot to piss in.

The other side had nothing, zero, less than zero.

I wasn't worried to begin with.

I was pissed.

I thought: too bad Del and me—we didn't crack the other two hooded radical protesters along with Rex Eagle.

Spin them out of their evil axis.

Or axis of evil.

Any way you want to put it.

Two less terrorists American taxpayers have to subsidize.

And a good way to release some of my leftover football rage.

It's legal and it beats the hell out of anger management classes.

**

Let me guess.

You are a… human shield.

Impelled by idealism, you insert your body between state-of-the-art war technology and its invested genocides.

Genocide is an abstraction.

Human Shield

These are innocents.
Children.
More than half the population is younger than five years old.

Five years there is not like five years here.
They mature fast in that climate.
What are you doing back up from Hades?

Raising funds for the Human Shield effort.
Not having much luck.
I'll be returning there in a few days.

What did you do before becoming a human shield?

I was a sword swallower

You swallowed swords?

Not just swords.
Cutlasses, rapiers, spears, shoulder-fired missiles, even tall wooden
staffs such as holy beggars used to carry.

Guess what.
Your holy beggars are back.
Except they call themselves opportunists.
Holy opportunists.
There's been one small change.
With the great forests obliterated, the beggars' staffs are no longer
constructed of wood.
Synthetics, friend.
Devised in our institutional laboratories.
Technology at work 24/7 to benefit every mother's son.
And daughter, of course.

I don't know what to say.

Bite your tongue.
Words, clauses, even your weightiest utterances are now fashioned electronically.
When was the last time you trolled the Net?

I couldn't tell you.

You must have been away a long time.

Ten months.

That's a lifetime, electronically speaking.
Speed, speed.
But just where are we heading?
Who cares.
Speed is its own excuse for being, right?

[Pause]

Speaking of opportunists, the fact is your holy opportunists no longer carry staffs at all.
They carry computers or printers, fax machines or scanners, high-definition TVs, cellphones, of course.
Everything cunningly miniaturized.
Did you know that your cellphone doubles as a palm pilot and missile launcher.
It also dispenses condoms and plays God Bless America.
In Esperanto.

I didn't know all that.

Well, you were gone for ten months, brother.
What did you do before you swallowed swords?

Venture capital.

Big dollars, right?

Depends on what you call big.

They say you can never be too rich.
Or too slim for that matter.
The slim part you've got covered.
Probably from being a human shield in your oppressed third world paradise.
Just about anything you eat or drink there is going to slip-slide through your gut and out the back vent.
No insult intended: When was the last time you had a good wash?

[Pause]

So you went from venture capital to sword swallowing to becoming a human shield in your infected third world country.

No.
After the sword swallowing I worked for Banana Republic.
After that I was a contract killer.

Cool.
What was your weapon of choice?
Semi-automatic? Machine pistol? Rocket-propelled grenade launcher? Plastique?

I used a six-inch buck knife.

Buck knife?
That's old school.
Plus it takes some muscle, which you don't have.
Well, you're a righteous, ascetic human shield.
You had to have been fitter back then than now.
You whack anyone interesting?
Let me rephrase that.
Did you whack anyone who didn't deserve whacking?

Can't say.
I don't think that way anymore.

You're a pacifist, right?

Non-violent activist is what we call it.

Euphonious.
What did you do after your stint as a contract killer?

Marine Corps.
I was involved in the first attempted genocide in '91.

We left that job undone, didn't we?
It's called compassion.
Which is why we're known world-wide as the white hats with the
big hearts.
You participated in Desert Storm, eh?

Jesus Disney is what we called it.

I know the drill.

You saw things there that troubled you.
Tweaked your conscience.
Curdled your tum.
Affected your sleep.
Encouraged you to question your middle-class values.
Feel guilty about the privileges our great country grants you.

Cluster bombs.

Tank plows that buried thousands of Iraqi troops alive.

Carpet bombing from above the cloud line which routinely missed intended targets and murdered civilians.

Collateral damage, right?

That's what they call it.

Depleted uranium used in missiles, bombs and high-caliber tank rounds.

Since 1991 the fallout from the radiation has killed massive numbers of people unconnected to the war.

In Basra, nearly 48 percent of the children suffer from terminal cancer.

It is much the same throughout the southern sectors of the country.

The US-sponsored embargo will not permit even the most basic hospital equipment to reach those tormented humans.

In 1991 British, Canadian and New Zealand commands protested the US's nuclear war.

The US rejected their protests out of hand.

The result was that a large number of British, Kiwis, and Canadians simply refused to fight.

Nervous Nellies.
The pale Brits can always use a boot in the ass from their brawnier cousins across the Atlantic.

Get their blood coursing.
The French are worse, but don't let me get started on that.
How many human shields do you have all together?

A few hundred.
New people keep joining.

Not just Americans, right?

Far from it.
Twenty—at least twenty—countries are represented.

Mostly young people, I expect.
Kid-idealists who've spent their brief lives surfing the Net and eating pizza.
Playing video games.
Indulged and isolated from real time.
From our ferocious, filthy, funked-over planet.

Not only young people.
I'm no longer young, obviously.
We have people in their sixties and seventies, male and female.
Christians, Buddhists, Muslims, Jews...

Jews too?
Way cool.
And you're all prepared to sacrifice your lives for your quixotic cause?
Because you know, don't you?, that the white hats will bomb your butts if they have to.
They sure as heck ain't about to cut and run.

Every Shield I've met is committed to staying the course.

And if you stay the course and lose your life?
What have you gained?
Martyrdom, Muslim style?
Seventy-two—or is it eighty-four?—supple, fragrant virgins and infinite hashish on the other side?

"Gain" is something we haven't discussed.
We hope to prevent the invasion and genocide of innocent humans.
Demonstrate to those under siege that we are friends, not enemies.

And you trust that your new-found friends will not betray you?

Betray us?
No.
We think we are recognized as friends in the name of peace.

You're a somber young man.
Actually, you're no longer young, as you've indicated.
You're sort of grim-faced, lined around the eyes.
As if you've seen the shit and resurfaced with a foul mouthful to bear witness.
For you and your kind there is no longer time or place for banter.
Not having an occasional laugh is like not having a good dump in the a.m.
It affects your health and tone and mood for the rest of the day.
Of course you're an idealist, maybe bordering on fanatic.
So not shitting is right up your alley.
I wish you luck in containing evil.
And best of luck after death with your eighty-four fragrant, acrobatic virgins.
Nirvana, Mecca, the martyred after-life.
Whatever these fanatical friends of yours call their outlandish heaven.

I'll give you some unasked-for advice, Mr. Human Shield.
Keep at least one sharp eye out for STD's.
In case you forgot, that stands for Sexually Transmitted Disease.
Wherever you're crashing in that god-forsaken place, never, ever leave your room, den, kennel, kraal, lair, burrow, gulag, kasbah, souk without two things.

[Pause]

You know what two things I mean, right?

The Good Book and a canteen of water?

No. No way, Shield.
A failsafe condom and a cellphone is what I'm talkin' about.
Just make sure the cell has a "global roaming" capability.
Whatever cave or kraal or ghetto you're stuck in anyplace on the globe, you'll always be able to call home.

Revolt Wives

R

A *lumpen* of frenzied dogs attacked a file of parked cars during the early dawn hours in the ancient Caribbean fortress city of Cartagena, Colombia, damaging the cars and causing panic among residents woken by the clamor, the police reported. Fenders, mud flaps, hubcaps and license plates were ripped away and windshields were shattered.

Car alarms screeched and wailed.

"It sounded like the cars were being broken into with a broadax," said Hugo Banzer, 36, one of several armed guards patrolling a seaside corporate office building.

"It was incredible. I watched three of the dogs leap again and again with unbelievable force into the side of one car, a white luxury Mercedes, biting and tearing at it like lunatics. Fortunately no passengers were in the cars. They would have been slaughtered."

Banzer said that he and the other armed guards shot at the assaulting dogs without hitting any of them.

After doing their damage, the dogs, still foaming with rage, backed away and slunk off into the night.

E

A *Gestapo* of frenzied dogs, including alsatians, rottweilers and doberman pinschers, attacked a line of parked cars in downtown Munich, damaging them and causing panic among shop owners, customers and residents, the police reported. Fenders, mud flaps, hubcaps, medallions and license plates were viciously ripped away and windshields were shattered.

Car alarms screeched and wailed.

"It sounded like the cars were being broken into with large hammers," said Wilhelm Frick, 38, a software engineer, who had been drinking and singing patriotic songs in a nearby beer garden.

"It was incredible. I watched three of them leap again and again with unbelievable force into the side of a large silver Mercedes sedan, tearing into it with their teeth.

"The odd thing is that these dogs were not rabble. They were very well-bred. And I could see they were not rabid. I can't imagine what possessed them.

"It is fortunate the assaulted cars were empty or else we would have had some torn-apart humans."

After wreaking their terror, the dogs, still foaming with rage, slunk off into the night.

V

A *kasbah* of frenzied dogs, including alsatians, presa canarios and feral black poodles, attacked a queue of parked cars during the early dawn hours, in Vichy, France, damaging them and causing panic among residents woken by the clamor, the police reported.

Fenders, mud flaps, hubcaps and license plates were ripped away and windshields were shattered.

Car alarms screeched and wailed.

"It sounded like the cars were being violently broken into with a broadax," said Pierre-Luc Pétain, 38, a functionary in the local government, who had been nursing a Calvados while reading *Le Figaro* and smoking *Gitanes Blondes* in a nearby cafe.

"It was incredible. I watched three of the dogs leap again and again with unbelievable force into the side of one car, a white luxury Citroën, biting and tearing at it like lunatics.

"The people at the tables outside scattered. I was inside the café but still felt unsafe. Fortunately nobody was in the assaulted cars; they would have been slaughtered."

After wreaking their terror, the dogs, still foaming with rage, slunk off into the night.

O

A *death row* of frenzied dogs, including boxers, rottweilers, pit bulls and doberman pinschers, broke into a large biotechnology complex in an elite outpost of Virginia, not far from the Capital, at dawn, and viciously attacked fourteen parked cars, damaging the cars and causing panic among the employees, the special police reported.

Though it was three-twenty a.m. on a Saturday in June, it was wartime and the biotech complex was humming.

The maddened dogs ripped fenders, flag decals, hubcaps and license plates from the cars and shattered windshields.

Car alarms screeched and wailed. At least one of the alarms resembled the melody of God Bless America, *in extremis*.

"To me it sounded like the cars were being assaulted with hammers and crowbars," said one of several heavily armed guards who refused to give his name.

"It was incredible. Three of the dogs leapt again and again with unbelievable force into the side of one car, a burgundy and white customized Lincoln, biting and tearing at it like lunatics. And these were obviously well-bred dogs, with pedigrees. Fortunately none of the managers were in their cars. They would have been ripped apart."

The armed guards fired at the assaulting dogs without hitting any of them.

After wreaking their terror, the dogs, still foaming with rage, backed away, leaped over the restraining walls or fences and faded back into the night.

L

A *Bantustan* of frenzied dogs, mutts and mixed breeds, broke into a gated seaside community at dawn in Cape Town, South Africa, and attacked a queue of nineteen parked cars, damaging them and causing panic among residents woken by the clamor, the government service reported.

Fenders, medallions, hubcaps and license plates were viciously ripped away and windshields were shattered. Car alarms screeched and wailed.

"It sounded like the cars were being assaulted with large hammers," said Hendrik Smuts, 38, one of the heavily armed resident guards.

"It was incredible. Three of the dogs leapt again and again with unbelievable force into the side of one car, a silver and white luxury Mercedes, biting and tearing at it like lunatics.

"The dogs were filthy feral mixed breeds but they did not look rabid. Fortunately none of the residents were in the cars. They would have been slaughtered."

Smuts reported that he and the other armed guards shot at the assaulting dogs without hitting any of them.

After wreaking their terror, the dogs, still foaming with rage, backed off, leaped over the restraining walls or fences and slunk back into the night.

T

A *Gaza* of frenzied dogs of indeterminate breeds, colored black and brown and spotted, somehow got into the walled, heavily guarded Mossad complex, in Tel Aviv and attacked eleven parked cars, damaging them and causing panic among Mossad officials whose first thought had to be: suicide bombers.

Mossad is the Israeli secret service, and though the dog assault took place in the early dawn hours on a Sunday in July, the complex, at work night and day throughout the year, was in full function.

Fenders, medallions, hubcaps and license plates were ripped away and windshields were shattered. Car alarms screeched and wailed.

"It sounded like the cars were being assaulted with large hammers," said one of the dozen or so armed guards who requested anonymity.

"It was incredible. Three of the dogs leapt again and again with unbelievable force into the side of one car, a silver and beige luxury Mercedes, biting and tearing at it like lunatics. The dogs were filthy mixed breeds, scavengers, but they did not look rabid. Fortunately none of our people were in the cars. They would have been mauled."

The armed guards shot at the assaulting dogs without hitting any of them.

After wreaking their terror, the dogs, still foaming with rage, backed away, leaped over the restraining walls and faded back into the night.

**

The reason I'm standing in the rain handing out *Bring-Our-Troops-Home* flyers is my son, Camilo.

He joined the Marine Corps to learn a trade.

He was seventeen.

He didn't join the Marine Corps to fight and get killed or poisoned in Iraq.

I gave him permission to join because in our neighborhood there was nothing for him but drugs and gangs.

I thought: better the Marines than prison.

Now I'm not so sure.

Now I'm thinking prison would be safer than Iraq.

My own brother Juan-Luis, he was there in '91 when the other Bush, the father, made war.

Juan-Luis—we call him Pepe—came back real sick with that Gulf War Syndrome, and he's still sick.

Headaches, sick to his stomach, high fevers.

Which is why he can't hold a steady job.

In the veteran's hospital they say they can't do anything about it.

Pepe's daughter, Amelia, she was born with leukemia, which the doctors, they wouldn't say anything, but I think it's because of what Pepe caught in the Gulf in '91.

Pepe says that a lot of poor Arabs, children too, who had nothing to do with the war were poisoned and have developed cancer.

Now it's happening all over again with Camilo.

First bomb a country to pieces, then rebuild it.

I just don't understand.

Camilo has been there for eleven months, in Iraq.

I am afraid for him.

I want him home.

Rosie Ruiz was in bed with a migraine at 7:25 on a Saturday morning when her seven-year-old daughter Rikki bounded into the room, screaming, "mommy, mommy, there's a man in uniform at the door."

Ruiz, the wife of a Marine Corps artillery sergeant stationed in Iraq, threw on a robe and dashed to the door, her head reeling:

He can't be dead. He can't be dead.

A Marine in full camouflage was at the door.

But he wasn't the messenger of death from the Department of Defense.

He was a neighbor locked out of his apartment a few doors down.

A gunnery sergeant named Junior Grissom transferred from Quantico to Twentynine Palms Marine Corps Combat Center, San Bernardino, CA.

Junior, his wife and baby moved into the on-base NCO units where the Ruiz family lived.

Just last week Bobbi Grissom told Rosie Ruiz in the laundromat that her husband had completed a tough ten months in Iraq and now was being shipped back.

Bobbi Grissom was real upset about that.

Rosey Ruiz is still upset.

The panic about her husband being killed in Iraq mostly passed, thanks to Paxil.

But not the migraines.

Not the anger that after spending fifteen months in Iraq her husband, Artillery Sergeant Pedro "Pete" Ruiz, has not come home, even though President Bush declared more than ten months ago that "major combat operations in Iraq have ended."

Anger that the Marine Corps has assigned dangerous new duties to her husband and his battalion that have nothing to do with toppling Saddam Hussein.

Anger that the talk in Washington and the media is not of taking troops out of Iraq, but of sending more in.

"I am so on edge," Mrs Ruiz, the mother of three small children, said.

"When him and the other men first left, I thought yeah, this will be bad, but war is what they trained for.

"But now they are not fighting a war.

"Not doing what they trained for.

"They have become police in a place they are hated and are the targets of assassins.

"I want my husband home."

Military families, accustomed to putting a cheery face on war, are growing vocal.

Since major combat for the 180,000 troops in Iraq was declared over on May 1, more than 300 Americans, including 83 killed in hostile encounters, have died in Iraq.

Those are the official estimates; many think the actual number of American fatalities is much, much higher.

Frustrations became so bad recently at Fort Stewart, Ga., that a colonel, meeting with 800 seething wives, had to be escorted from the session.

"They were crying, cussing, yelling and screaming for their men to come back," said Deirdre Dixon, director of community services at Fort Stewart.

The signs of discomfort seem to be growing beyond the military bases. According to a Gallup poll published on Tuesday, the percentage of the public who think the war is going badly has risen to 49 percent, from 13 percent in May.

Likewise, the number of respondents who think the war is going well has dropped, from 86 percent in May to 70 percent six weeks ago to 39 percent as of today.

The latest poll was based on cellular phone interviews with 1,003 adult citizens.

It has a sampling error of plus or minus three percentage points.

Despite the administration's feverish attempts at damage control, flooding the media with feel-good stories about the successes in Iraq and the Middle East, the actual news this week has not helped.

Thursday, nine American soldiers were killed in a terrorist explosion and another seven were hurt in hit-and-run attacks, which concluded with an enraged crowd of Iraqis stomping and spitting on a burned-out Humvee.

"Our soldiers were supposed to be welcomed by waving crowds.

"Where did those waving crowds go?" said Kim Leftwich, whose husband is part of a Camp Lejeune-based Marine Corps artillery unit, 3-16 Bravo, known as the Barracuda.

In the so-called postwar and pre-peace phase, it is not Green Berets or top-gun fighter pilots who are being killed.

The casualties have been mostly low-ranking ground troops performing mundane activities like buying a video, going out on patrol or guarding a trash pit.

Those are the types of missions the Barracuda are on.

With major battles over for the time being and little use for field cannon with uranium rounds that can shoot 15 miles and penetrate reinforced concrete, the Barracuda have been running checkpoints and searching houses north of Baghdad, rarely firing a shell, while dodging deadly booby-traps and ambushes.

The Barracuda took up their assignment in April along with 20,000 other Marines from Camp Lejeune, N.C.

Yellow ribbons now droop from the magnolia trees where they used to meet at dawn to stretch and do pushups.

The grass is rank and overgrown.

The blacktop that once echoed with roll call and the stomp of a thousand combat boots is hot, quiet and empty.

Marine Corps bases can be drab places in the best of times.

Camp Lejeune right now is downright depressing.

Even on the Fourth of July.

"I tried every trick in the book to get us out of this," admitted Colonel Rory Piersall, the commander of the rear detachment for the artillery soldiers who have remained in Camp Lejeune.

"But orders are orders."

There is not much glory in helping single mothers have their cars repaired or overseeing insurance benefits.

But that is the work of the officers and NCOs left behind in Camp Lejeune, Twentynine Palms and in the other mostly deserted Marine Corps bases in the US.

"The anxiety level is way up there," Colonel Piersall said.

Fourteen Marines from Camp Lejeune and eleven from Twentynine Palms have been killed in Iraq in the last six weeks.

More and more wives and mothers are dreading that knock on the door.

And there are other worries.

War can find the weakest seam of a military marriage and split it open. After the Persian Gulf war, divorce rates at military bases shot up as much as 50 percent, an army study showed.

"That's my biggest fear," said Valerie-Jean Tejada, the wife of a Marine Corps lance corporal in Iraq.

"That my husband will come back different or sick.

"Even if you're G.I. Joe, if you have to kill someone, that's not something you just forget about."

Mrs Tejada is stumped about what to do when the doorbell rings and her 19-month-old son Adam runs to answer, saying, "Dada, dada."

"What do I tell him?" she asked.

Monique Ledbetter, wife of a Marine Corps gunnery sergeant with the Barracuda unit, said her toddler daughter threw a tantrum the other day, saying she wanted to eat pizza on the floor "with daddy."

And Mrs Ledbetter keeps having the same nightmare.

"I am wheeling my stroller with my daughter Marni on a deserted freeway, and suddenly I see Johnny, my husband, clear as day.

"He is in combat uniform, slumped behind the wheel of a burning car or tank, and he doesn't even raise his head when I wave and shout to him.

"In the dream he is alive but very depressed and is hiding from me and our daughter out of shame.

"Shame for what he is doing over there."

Besides the other fatalities from Camp Lejeune, six Barracuda have been killed in guerrilla incidents since they were re-deployed in Iraq five weeks ago.

All the Barracuda wives seem to be bracing for the worst.

"'Names pending release, names pending release'—I hate that expression," Valerie-Jean Tejada said of the way the military announces casualties and being told who they are.

The wives at both Twentynine Palms and Camp Lejeune console themselves by making bracelets for their husbands and sending care packages.

Monique Ledbetter included a Best Buy circular in a recent box at her husband's request.

Summer Thomasson shipped the latest issue of Parents magazine, but not at her husband's request.

Summer Thomasson is seven months pregnant and married to an artillery sergeant.

"Whether he likes it or not, he's coming back a daddy," she said with a rueful smile.

Great efforts are made to stay upbeat.

On a recent day, a group of Barracuda wives chatted in Monique Ledbetter's living room, nibbling corn chips and sipping Pepsi Lites.

But things are becoming more intense, they said.

The widening chaos in Iraq means their husbands will stay longer, and the women do not need a poll to tell them that public opinion is shifting.

"When my husband first deployed, the people at work were so sweet, giving me days off, saying take whatever time I need," recalled Summer Thomasson, who answers telephones at a financial institution near Camp Lejeune.

"But it's not like that now.

"Now they look at me kind of funny and say: 'Why do you need a day off now?

"'Isn't the war over?'"

Mother Palestine

Tell me, why do they do this?

Why do they blow up your house?
To root out fanatical Muslim insurgents.

My son is twelve years old.

Brown children living in desert climates grow fast.
If they are Muslim zealots they grow fast and violent.
Toddlers are instructed to hate and inflict murder on the greatest
number while shattering themselves.
After their martyr's death they are reassembled and granted bounti-
ful rewards in the Islamic afterworld.
So the fanatical doctrine decrees.

[Pause]

In mother Europe, not so long ago, every Jew, young or old, was
thought to be a Communist or a traitor.
Today every Arab is an insurgent.
In his own country.
They claim the insurgents use the small houses on the perimeter to
shoot at their troops.
Fire home-made Qassam rockets at innocent Israelis over the border.

My son goes to school.
He does not shoot rockets.

They claim that when the fanatical insurgents are not shooting and firing Qassam rockets, they pray to Allah.

After praying they throw stones.

A stone well-placed can penetrate an armored bulldozer.

Penetrate an advancing tank.

Bring down a helicopter gunship.

When the fanatical insurgents are not throwing stones they are digging tunnels from the small houses on the perimeter to the command and control sector in the refugee camp's interior.

Refugee?
Is that what we have become in our own land?

They claim the insurgents are using the tunnels to smuggle weapons from the Egyptian border to the Gaza refugee camp.

Even as they themselves were not so long ago despised refugees in their own towns and cities throughout mother Europe.

They demolished our home and everything my family has ever had.
Now we have nothing.

Not so long ago they were sealed into ghettos in mother Europe.

Those not murdered were packed into "cattle cars," transported to the death camps.

Now they claim that after the massive demolitions their army engineers will dig a deep moat between the Gaza perimeter and the Egyptian border.

The demolitions of Palestinian homes and the deep moat lining the border will create a "new reality" on the border between Gaza and Egypt.

Those Palestinians who manage to get to Egypt for whatever reason will not be permitted back in Gaza.

[Pause]

Not so long ago Propaganda Minister Goebbels proclaimed the commencement of a "new reality."

Goebbels was the libidinous smaller half of the Goering & Goebbels vaudeville duo.

Mammoth pink Goering, Air Minister of the Luftwaffe, opium eater.

"Fat Pink," as he was called behind his back, gleefully played the horse's ass.

Goebbels with his pointed snout played the horse's head.

They were the Nazi equivalent of Laurel and Hardy, whom we viewed in the darkened movie theaters and laughed at during that bleak, irreal time.

I do not understand.

The so-called buffer zone separating your "camp" from the engagement area at the border is currently 200 meters wide.

The assaulting forces plan to widen it to 300 meters.

Which means demolishing homes which are relatively interior, already separated from the engagement area, uninvolved in the insurgency.

Why can't they leave us in peace?

They call it defensive strategy.

It could be they intend to annex Gaza.

Not so long ago in mother Europe the sovereign nation of Austria was annexed.

Smug Habsburg Vienna, with its Mozart, *Ringstrasse*, bulbous baroque monuments to smugness and rich pastries with cream—every last morsel sucked into the Nazi swirl.

Already set in motion was the million-fold genocide they called the "final solution."

Who called?
The Israelis?

The Nazis, Mother.

I'm unearthing pertinent recent history.

Though it occurred on a different continent.

Like the pendulum of a giant clock, before enforced digitalization, I'm lurching back and forth in time, from continent to bleeding continent.

In the three and a half years since the Intifada, Amnesty International estimates that the assaulting forces have demolished more than 3,000 Palestinian homes.

Tens of thousands left homeless.

[Pause]

Now the assaulting forces intend to seal off your camp to prevent insurgents from slipping out among the fleeing civilians.

Non-combatants like yourself who have had their small houses demolished.

It is much harder to flee now that their army has broken up the only road with bulldozers.

It will be almost impossible to cross the border into Egypt once the deep moat is in place.

We do not cross into Egypt.
Our home is here.

They claim that the massive demolitions do not represent "ethnic cleansing."

Nor was European Jewry *vermin* even when branded and sealed into ghettos throughout much of mother Europe.

This is not Europe.

With respect, Mother, it is and it isn't.

Not so long ago the human disease took hold in the European continent and metastasized with unimaginable rapidity.

The center collapsed, the world was sucked irresistibly into the swirl.

Black, sightless.

Now and here the center has collapsed again.

God is our center.
Our faith in our God.

[Pause]

Is there no one to help you and your family?
No UN-sponsored agency?
No International Red Cross?

There are too many of us now homeless.
With nothing.
We must help each other.

Where do you and your family sleep?

It is just my husband and me.
We sleep in a small tent near our mosque.
Tents with families from demolished homes you see in and around
all the mosques.

[Pause]

Is your son arrested?

Thank God, no.
I sent him to my brother in Jordan.
If he was here they would arrest him.
Or murder him.

They claim the arrests and assassinations are purely defensive.

To protect their troops and army posts from fanatical suicidal terrorists.

Demonstrate a firm hand to the insurgents who are also the terrorists.

Do what needs to be done to maintain a fragile peace in the area.

Peace we had before they came and murdered our children.
Demolished our homes.

They claim the massive demolitions are not war crimes.

That they have nothing to do with "ethnic cleansing."

Nor did "Kristallnacht" in 1938, the violent assault on Jewish-owned shops and businesses, the smashing of the windows of those establishments, the beatings and execution of the Jewish inhabitants.

They have demolished our homes.
Now we have nothing.

Permit me to tell you something, Mother.

The cattle cars, the so-called concentration camps, the sinister medical experiments, the ovens, the massive pyramids of shoes, the million-fold genocide, the final solution.

It is a monstrous lie perpetrated by Zionists and fellow travelers.

You've heard the Zionist slogan: Never Again.

It is a fabrication, a lie.

A "chosen people" perpetuating their own tragic myth.

Among other things, it validates Jewish chronic mass hysteria.

The Holocaust, with a capital "H", never happened, you see.

And so long as we possess memory it will never happen among civilized nations.

We have nothing.
Nothing.

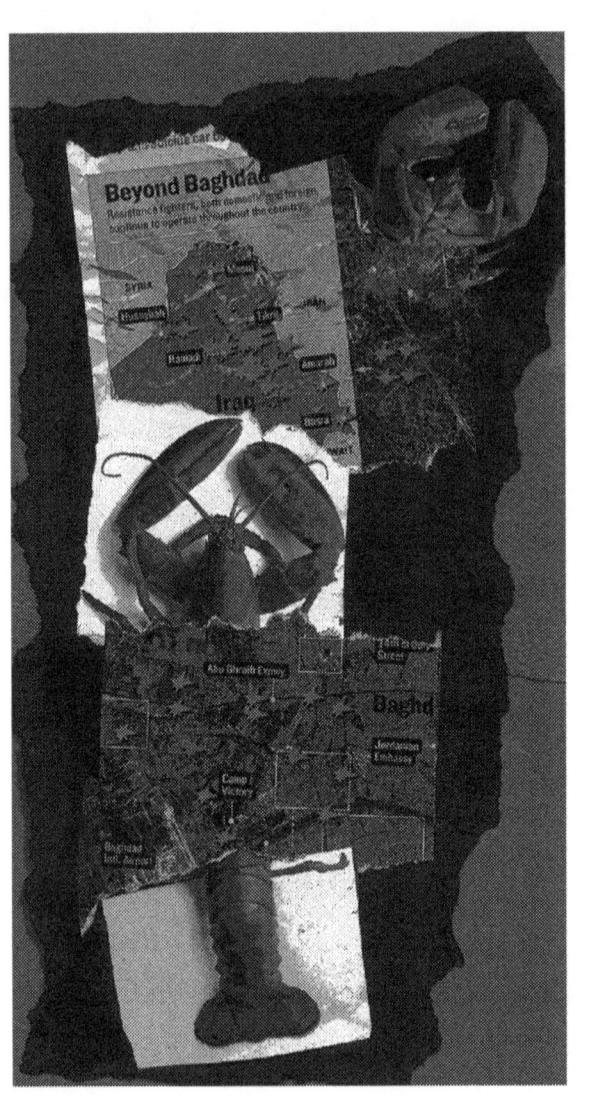

Baghdad Barbershop

As soon as the images of Uday and Qusay Hussein came into blurry focus on the ancient Zenith round-screen TV, an argument erupted in the cramped Abu Ahmad Barbershop in devastated downtown Baghdad.

The barbershop smelled pungently of sweet hair tonic and strong tobacco, and the six variously aged Iraqi males stood or squatted while the barber shaved his customer in one of the two barber's chairs.

The second barber's chair was piled with cartons and old newspapers and the TV set was mounted high in a corner of the shop away from the window.

Half the men, it seemed, exulted that their former oppressors were dead, while the others dismissed the pictures as American forgeries.

The Bush administration, after an intense debate about cultural sensitivities and military ethics, had decided to release the pictures in full gruesome detail to convince a fretful, war-torn Iraqi populace that the two demon sons of a demonically autocratic leader were actually dead.

A civilian spokesman for the occupying authority who requested anonymity said that many Saddam-brutalized Iraqis remained so nervous about a comeback by the ruthless Hussein dynasty that they would believe any conspiracy theory to that effect.

"Right now a lot of these folks are in denial," the anonymous spokesman said.

"So it's up to us to take steps to reassure them, to reiterate the point we made from the get-go, that the bad guys are never, ever coming back.

"At least for as long as we're calling the shots."

Two senior members of the eight-member Iraqi Governing Council, all of whom were invited to view the actual bodies, advised their colonizers that they should clean and shave the corpses' faces, since having them look more like themselves would be reassuring to the Iraqi public.

On the other hand, many Baghdadis appeared distinctly blasé about the whole thing, thumping melons or haggling over the price of kabobs in the busy shopping district of Karada without even glancing up at the grisly images spooling past every few minutes on the giant billboard-size TV set.

Exhibited on the TV were two pairs of photos: *Left*, the living, grinning, clean-shaven Hussein brothers: Uday in a shirt and polka dot bowtie and Qusay in traditional Arab robe and headdress; *Right*, the shirtless upper torsos of the two battered, bloated corpses, their heavy beards matted with congealed blood.

Each was evidently lying on the hardened desert earth, Uday in what seemed to be an unzipped, olive drab, bloodstained body bag,

Behind Uday's distended corpse, a human hand in a pink glove pointed to a white cloth on which were arranged certain objects.

The camera then zoomed in to reveal a Kalashnikov assault rifle; a prescription-size container with the single word **Viagra** stamped on it; a cardboard packet of Trojan spermicidal condoms labeled "Jumbo Size"; three DVDs, only one of which had a legible title: "Hardcore Hotties"; and a narrow glass vial half-filled with white powder.

A metal bucket of sudsy water sat nearby.

Qusay's corpse was shown lying on a pile of soiled sheets, his grotesquely swollen face to the side and his bloody, toothless mouth agape.

Both men had their eyes closed.

Uday, 39, had the most damaged features, with the area around his upper lip mangled and a long bruise trailing from his mouth across his face.

A purplish, uneven, star-shaped wound blossomed on the right side of the stubble of his shaved head.

An American military spokesman, Brig. General Hoyt Teasley, rejected out of hand allegations that Uday had committed suicide, that he was severely tortured, or that the corpse was not Uday to begin with.

Two days earlier, a junior military spokesman, Major Terry Rayburn, said that a complete match to Uday's dental records was not possible because his jaw was fractured and 70 percent of his teeth were shattered.

Regarding the fact that the corpses looked much fatter than the live images of the brothers, Major Rayburn attributed that to their "decadent lifestyle."

Autopsies to confirm the cause of death had not been completed.

The two despotic sons of Saddam were reportedly killed Tuesday after an Iraqi tipped off American forces that they were hiding in a house in the northern city of Mosul, their Russian-made Kalashnikov automatic rifles falling silent after American troops fired 93 antitank missiles at the house.

The Iraqi informer whose identity was not revealed for fear of recriminations was now at an undisclosed location waiting impatiently to claim his seven million dollar "dead or alive" reward.

US authorities were reportedly trying to ascertain whether the informer actually fulfilled all of the stipulations of the reward.

The newspaper photos of the two corpses were closely scrutinized by the men in the barber shop, and there was whistling and clucking when the televised images appeared on the main 9 pm newscast.

The arguments began raging immediately, reflecting all the rumors and skepticism with which Iraqis filter any announcements from their new colonial rulers.

"In a few days they will show us another fat body with a beard and say it's Saddam himself," said Zohair Maty, a 35-year-old laborer.

"We all knew Uday was a playboy, but why would he be carrying

Viagra, porno videos and cocaine?" 23-year-old Khalid Sirhan Muhammad wondered.

"Why would he even need Viagra?" Zohair Maty added with a sly grin. "To me the Americans staged the whole thing, overdoing it so that everyone would be sure to see how degenerate Uday is."

"You don't believe he is really dead, then?" the lathered-faced man in the barber's chair asked.

At that moment, the conversation was interrupted by the rat-a-tat-tat of what sounded like celebratory gunfire.

Arabs have the unnerving habit of shooting their guns into the air at even the smallest pretext.

"It's the first time I ever saw Iraqi people happy because brother Iraqis were murdered," shouted the barber, Abu Ahmad, who with his straight razor continued to shave his customer's throat through the gunfire.

Several of the men shook their heads or clucked in agreement.

Of the eight humans in the cramped barbershop, an informal tally suggested that three were now convinced they recognized Saddam Hussein's sons in the battered, bloated corpses and five were doubtful.

The men look much too fat, one said.

They were not burned the way the first news reports said they were, another said.

Abu Ahmad, the barber, seemed to waver.

"From the features on their face, I would say it is probably them," he said.

Then, pointing with his razor to the live and dead face of Qusay in the open newspaper, he added: "His dead left ear doesn't seem the same as his alive left ear."

"If it had been me I would have shaved their beards before showing them," the lathered man in the barber's chair said.

"It is just not right to display them that way."

The conversation then segued from the authenticity of the photos to the bravery of Saddam's sons in fighting against a reported 1,500 American soldiers with helicopter gunships, missiles, tanks and highly toxic depleted uranium.

Two of the men expressed anger that the Americans stripped the Iraqi flags from the graves of Uday and Qusay Hussein.

At their funeral, the red, white and black flags were laid on the stone mounds above their bodies, alongside the grave of Mustafa Hussein, Qusay's 14-year-old son, who was killed when the American troops attacked the Mosul villa in which the brothers were allegedly hiding two weeks ago. ***

The brothers themselves escaped only to be hunted down and killed in another Mosul villa a week later.

That was the American occupier's version.

Now the Americans allowed only the murdered child's remains to be honored with his country's flag.

Uday and Qusay had no memorial save for the heavy footprints of US Army boots.

Between exhibiting the corpse photos and commercial messages, the Iraqi network (run now by the American occupiers) broadcast a video-tape showing a grinning Uday in what looked like pictures from a dozen years ago, dancing with numerous young women, sometimes two and three at a time, at a palace disco.

Every one of the women wore a leather or vinyl miniskirt.

"How come they're all wearing miniskirts?" the man in the barber's chair wondered.

"You'd rather have them wearing nothing at all," someone else laughed.

"If only I had robbed a bank, I would have a big Mercedes," said Akeel Umran, a 23-year-old laborer. "I would then fire my Kalashnikov at the sky, and bring all those girls in their leather miniskirts to my house."

After a brief pause someone mentioned the Iraqi army that was routed by the US invaders in the recent, rapid war which the Americans declared won but which continued with even more ferocity.

Which provoked a few of the younger men to breathe a sigh of relief that the arrival of the Americans meant they would not be forced to perform military service—or pay a bribe that would end up in Uday's pocket to avoid being conscripted.

When one young man criticized the occupation, noting that the Americans had not added so much as a bar of soap to the monthly government rations that most Iraqis have been living on for so long, his friend shot back: "As long as we are free from military service, I can do without soap for the rest of my life."

There was further grumbling that the sons of a president should not die that way, even if they had oppressed the Iraqi people.

One man suggested it was a sad thing any time Muslims are killed by outsiders.

"I hope they are not dead," the barber, Abu Ahmad, said while toweling off the face of his customer.

"What are you talking about? I want them butchered, slaughtered like the beasts they are," said his brother Yasir, who that minute entered the shop making a slit throat gesture with his finger.

As closing time neared, the conversation swirled back to whether the deaths really would improve the lives of Iraqis.

In any case, that would be the customers' last glimpse of the mutilated corpses, at least for the night, since the shop lost its electricity every night by 9:30 p.m.

Which was still better than under the brutal reign of Saddam when lights would go out at 8:45 at the latest.

**

According to a declaration from the United Nations Urgent Aid

Organization (UAO), a plague of desert locusts could soon hit several north African states.

1) This year's locust swarm is likely to be in the trillions, which would make it the most massive locust pestilence in at least a century.

2) Individual swarms are expected to measure nine square miles in size and contain up to 60 million locust adults in each square mile of swarm.

3) The Desert Locust (*Schistocerca gregaria*) is one of about a dozen species of short-horned grasshoppers (*Acridoidea*) that are known to change their behavior and form swarms of adults or bands of hoppers (wingless nymphs).

4) The swarms that form are both extraordinarily dense and highly mobile.

5) During quiet periods (known as recessions), Desert Locusts are restricted to the semi-arid and arid deserts of Africa, the Near East and Southwest Asia that receive less than 200 mm of rain annually. This is an area of about 10 million square miles, consisting of about 30 countries.

6) During plagues, Desert Locusts may spread over an area of up to 40 million square miles, extending over 70 countries. This amounts to more than 30% of the total land surface of the world.

7) Desert Locusts fly with the wind at speeds between 16-23 mph.

8) Swarms can travel about 120 miles or more in a day.

9) Desert Locusts are capable of remaining in the air for extended periods of time. For example, the creatures regularly cross the Red Sea, a distance of 220 miles.

10) A Desert Locust adult can consume roughly its own weight in fresh food, which amounts to about two grams every day.

11) A very small part of an average swarm (approximately one ton of locusts) eats the same amount of food in one day as 70 camels, 30 elephants or 6,000 humans.

12) The UAO issued its first warning of a coming locust plague in February, when unusually high rates of breeding were detected

south of the Atlas Mountains in Morocco and Algeria.

13) Major insecticide spraying programs were initiated at once, with the aim of cutting the plague off at the source.

14) They have not been able to stem the tide.

15) The UAO says the first swarms of locusts have moved from their spring breeding grounds into Egypt, Libya, Morocco, and Algeria.

16) Mali, Niger, Chad and the Darfur region of Sudan will also see swarms in the next few weeks.

17) Most of those regions already suffer from malnutrition, selective starvation, fierce tribal conflicts, even civil wars.

18) A full-scale assault by the Desert Locust would amount virtually to genocide.

19) During plagues, the Desert Locust has the potential to damage the livelihood of a fifth of the world's population.

20) Unlike the 17 year cycle of the cicada, desert locust plagues develop intermittently.

21) Plagues of locusts have been reported since the Babylonian empire, in 2000 B.C.

22) During the 20th century, Desert Locust plagues occurred at the turn of the century, 1933-1946 and 1963-1973.

23) None of those outbursts are expected to be comparable to the massiveness of the coming plague.

24) About nine million dollars have been pledged for assistance, which the UAO insists is "woefully inadequate."

25) Not just more money but "infinitely more resources are urgently needed," according to the UAO.

26) Summer rains have already begun in the affected areas, which means the creatures will lay more eggs as they travel.

Here are a few local recipes from traditionally locust-affected countries. Please send us yours.

Tinjiya (Tswana recipe): Remove the wings and hind legs of the locusts and boil in water until soft. Add salt, if desired, and a little fat and fry until brown. Serve with cooked, dried mealies (corn).

Sikonyane (Swazi recipe): Prepare embers and roast the whole locust on the embers. Remove head, wings, and legs, since only the breast part is eaten. The South Sotho people use locusts especially as food for travelers. The heads and last joint of the hind legs are broken off and the rest laid on the coals to roast. The roasted locusts are ground on a grinding stone to a fine powder. This powder can be retained for a long time, hence can be taken on a journey. Dried locusts are also prepared for the winter months. The legs, when dried, are especially relished for their savory taste.

Cambodia: Take several dozen locust adults, preferably females, slit the abdomen lengthwise and stuff an unsalted peanut inside. Then lightly grill the locusts in a wok or hot frying pan, adding a little oil and salt to taste. Be careful not to overcook or burn them.

Mali: Prepare the embers or charcoal. Place about one dozen locusts on a skewer, stabbing each through the center of the abdomen. If you only want to eat the abdomen, then you may want to remove the legs or wings either before or after cooking. Several skewers of locusts may be required for each person. Place the skewers above the hot embers and grill while turning continuously until they become golden brown.

White Terror

Weight Loss

Undernourished mice created in an Atlanta genetics lab may offer hints at why some people can eat all they want and still stay thin.

Researchers have found that with a single genetic alteration they can turn up the natural metabolic furnace in mice so that the animals burn more fat. Experts said that people might soon be able to control their weight by doing the same thing, or by exploiting related processes.

Mice with the mutation have about 6% body fat, compared to about 15% in their unaltered brethren. But even more impressive, the genetically altered mice can eat a high-fat diet without ill effects.

*

Who would you bomb in that one?

I'd bomb the "experts."

I'd bomb the incorporated biotech firms that employ the "experts."

What about the genetically altered mice?

I'd grow them vampire teeth then drop them down the trousers of the corporate chieftains.

Smiling with Cancer

A man who for three years pretended to be dying of cancer—even shaving his head and faking seizures—got 14 months in prison Thursday. Kurt Kelleher, 50, was also ordered to repay nearly $43,000 to his victims and perform 200 hours of community service.

The former vacuum cleaner salesman claimed to have kidney, lung and prostate cancer. His former wife and three stepsons believed him, as did most of his fellow residents of Canterbury, a town of about 1,700 in central New Hampshire.

To convince people, Kelleher shaved his head, talked about how awful chemotherapy was and dropped red dye in his toilet to make it appear like blood in his urine.

"He also faked seizures, sometimes slamming his head into walls to make the episodes look realistic," said Branford Rawson, a federal prosecutor.

*

Who would you bomb in that one?

I'd bomb Branford Rawson, the federal prosecutor.

Hell, he's just a custodian with an Ivy League name. I'd bomb the federal judiciary building, in DC.

What about Kurt Kelleher, cancer lover?

I'd bust him out of jail, pin the coyote medal on his heart, and plant a wet kiss on his thin lips.

Pigeons

Several hundred pigeons were distributed to Marine Corps units in Baghdad to warn the leathernecks of chemical or biological attacks.

Like the canaries that miners once carried in case they ran into explosive gas underground, the pigeons fall victim to dangers and die.

In this instance, the pigeons are gassed or biologically infected by those predators with identical black mustaches.

Lacking our elevated moral nature (19th century term), pigeons die more rapidly than humans.

Lacking our far superior cerebral cortex, pigeons cannot experience pain like humans.

Marine Corps units, then, will get a heads-up from the suffocated-to-death pigeons.

The Marines will also be equipped with $682,000 worth of mechanical sensors in case the pigeons don't die on cue.

The pigeons cost $63 each, including seed.

*

Who would you bomb in that one?

I'd bomb the corporate think-tank that came up the stratagem of sacrificing pigeons.

What about the Marine Corps four-star general who passed down the order?

Court-martial his ass.

No shit. Dude will leave the Corps and get a job in industry paying him seven times what he got as a leatherneck.

Then interrogate him with extreme prejudice, along with the corporate think-tank humans. Do to them what's been done to their prisoners in Abu Ghraib and Guantánamo and the rest of those places where Muslim captives are "outsourced."

Who exactly are these "corporate think-tank humans" of which you speak?

Corgi

Queen Elizabeth was said to be devastated by the death of one of her corgis, put down after it was savaged by an English bull terrier belonging to her daughter, Princess Anne, newspapers reported.

The bull terrier, Dottie, which last year caused the princess to be fined after it severely bit two Pakistani children at a London park, attacked the queen's corgi, Raj, at a family gathering at Sandringham, the Sun reported.

The Daily Mail said that an elite veterinarian team was called in, but too late, and Raj, the corgi, one of the queen's oldest pets, was put to sleep.

*

Well?

I'd bomb the Englishman who invented the phrase "put down."

You assume it was an Englishman, and the probability is you're right. I would bomb the royal palaces, Windsor, Buckingham, those in Wales and Scotland, the lot.

And the Pakistani children severely bitten by Raj, the bull terrier?

No, Raj is the name of the corgi. Dottie is the bull terrier.

Sorry. What about the assaulted Pakistani children?

Bleach their skin and teach them to ride to hounds. If that doesn't take, send them back to Pakistan. As someone knowledgeable put it:

Since the death of Communism the ideological rift is no longer between West and East: freedom and totalitarianism; but between North and South: the exalted mores of Christian-Judaic culture as against the heat-scarred, emotion-laden Muslim sectors.

Hippo

Diana Silk-Davies, Ms South Africa in 2002 and first runner-up in the 2003 Ms World contest, was mauled by a hippopotamus while canoeing in Okavango swamp, Botswana, the local constabulary reported.

The blonde beauty winner, who was bitten on her face and thighs, was airlifted to Johannesburg hospital, where she was reported to be in critical condition.

Earlier this month, another South African beauty contest winner, Annette Jeanne Kruger, was murdered by a hippo while she and her family were on safari holiday in the Okavango.

*

The hippos are pissed.

Yes, they are. Who would you bomb?

She was a blonde Ms South Africa who was mauled by a hippo in Botswana. Where's Botswana?

North of South Africa. British colony until 1966. Former name: Bechuanaland.

Can we bomb the colonizing British retroactively?

Regrets, that isn't permitted.

I'd bomb blonde beauty contest winners who live and thrive in Africa with hyphenated surnames.

Me? I'd bomb the safari tourist trade.

Why did I expect you to say that? Which hand do you wipe your arse with?

Which hand? The left. The decisive blows are always struck left-handed.

Stoolmaker = Ayliffe

The families of two 17-year-old girls critically injured in separate car wrecks kept vigil at the wrong bedside for more than a week before one of the girls woke up and ended the confusion.

"Apparently, the two girls involved were the same age, had the same color eyes, both were unconscious, and both had swollen features," Gasland Hospital Superintendent Glenn Garver explained.

Oddly, each of the girls had a pet cat of the same species, a snowshoe female, which is half Siamese and half American shorthair.

The family of Lissa-Jean Stoolmaker watched over a girl in Gasland, a Flint hospital, for eight days before she regained consciousness Thursday and uttered her name: Jamie-Lynn Ayliffe, as well as her Social Security number and birthday.

Lissa-Jean Stoolmaker, it turned out, was in critical condition at Dogstar Hospital in Saginaw, Michigan, where Jamie-Lynn Ayliffe's family had been keeping watch.

*

Who would you bomb in that one?

I'd bomb the Michigan auto industry.

I'd bomb Gasland and Dogstar.

I'd bomb the nuclear family.

What about the all-American teenagers?

Bomb their butts.

All of 'em? Even the introverted ones who still dream, who don't dress hip-hop, play video games, gun their parents' SUVs?

Fuck yeah. If I don't bomb 'um I freeze 'um. Deep freeze. Cryonics.

And the bombed teens' cats ? The snowshoes?

Oh, spare the cats. Honor the cats. Snowshoes, Maine Coons, Rag Dolls, Persians, American shorthairs, Abyssinians, all of them. Erect a cantilevered city, plant artificial mice.

Sorry White Trash

In a profanity-ridden letter to the US Supreme Court, convicted murderer Rodney Mohammed Abu-Rauf admitted killing two young Taco Bell employees in Burbank, California, said he felt no remorse for the crimes, and demanded to be executed.

"I'm guilty as s---!" said the letter, signed by Rauf. "Ain' got no remorse! Give me my execution date and off me!"

Rauf, 35, is scheduled to be executed January 26 at Corcoran State Prison. The Compton man was convicted of fatally shooting a 27-year-old Taco Bell manager and a 16-year-old employee during a 2002 robbery that netted him about $111.

In Rauf's letter, released by the Supreme Court on Thursday, he addressed the high court judges as "sorry white trash plus one oreo," and demanded that they let him be executed, protesting against several appeals filed on his behalf in recent years by public defense attorneys.

In an earlier letter to the court, Rauf admitted stabbing one of his since disavowed attorneys 17 times at Corcoran, adding: "Unfortunately the piece of s--- lives."

Prison officials confirmed that Rauf did stab a lawyer multiple times with a pencil.

*

Isn't his name Abu-Rauf? How come they call him Rauf?

Because his real name is nigger black subhuman.

He stabbed his public defense lawyer 17 times with a pencil. He must have a hard fast stroke.

He's a strong guy, an athlete. Played defensive back for his community college football team before dropping out of school.
So who would you bomb?

I'd bomb Taco Bell and the fast food industry.

I'd bomb the industries that make a profit out of prison labor.

You'll need a whole lot of TNT for that deal. What about the government sectors responsible for the so-called obscenity statutes?

You mean for forcing folks to spell shit with an "s" and three dashes?

Uh-huh.

Shit, I'd bomb their sorry motherfucking asses back to the stone age.

Ain't that a little extreme?

Das right, Massa.

Sewage

Raw

Maybe it wasn't on the order of splitting the atom. Or spanning cables over the Pacific Ocean to construct the Golden Gate Bridge. Or erecting the ill-fated World Trade towers in downtown New York City.

But it was an engineering triumph all the same, thanks to the designated contractor: global giant Bechtel Corporation; the facilitator: the United States Agency for International Development (USAID); and the hands-on folks: the US Army Corps of Engineers, supplemented of course by native workers.

Yet when it was completed on October 31, Halloween, the achievement remained cloaked in secrecy, marked only by a low-key celebration among Bechtel executives and invited senior US Army and Marine Corps officers sipping California Chardonnay in a heavily guarded, undisclosed location.

What was this great engineering achievement?

A raw sewage processing plant.

Raw sewage, thousands and thousands of tons of the muck, was at long last going to be treated in the armpit of the world.

Baghdad, Iraq.

Cooked

So how long have you been an "interrogator"?

I was in the police force in Texarkana—

Texarkana, Texas or Texakarna, Arkansas?

Texas. Northeast Texas. From the police force I enlisted and asked for the MP's. Army Military Police. This was during Desert Storm.

From the MPs I moved into Intelligence, then Interrogation. Where I'm at now.

You've served in at least three of the US's detention camps: Guantánamo Bay, Diego Garcia and Bagram, Afghanistan.

Somebody briefed you good.

Raw

The Bechtel-treated water that eventually wound its way into the Tigris River was, relatively speaking, hardly more than a trickle.

It came to roughly 10 million gallons a day from a city that produces raw sewage at something like 40 times that rate.

Which, to give you an index of comparison, is 60 times the rate of New York City and 30 times the rate of one of the most polluted cities on planet earth, Calcutta, India.

Nonetheless, the "trickle" of treated water may be viewed as a kind of industrial miracle in a city where sewage plants have been so run-down and neglected that for the last 20 years each drop and dollop of human and subhuman waste was dumped untreated into the once-venerable Tigris River, fouling everything from essential dams to shorelines to drinking water systems downstream.

Care for a lethal dose of cholera or typhus?

Then fill your glass with Baghdad tap water.

Skoal, sucker!

Cooked

Your specific job is interrogation. Forcible interrogation, if necessary. You like the work?

Like, not-like. It's got to be done.

So you do it dutifully. As a patriot.

Is that tape running?

Tape is always running. Let me ask you this. The 1949 Geneva Convention requires prisoners of war to be read the charges against them and to have access to legal counsel. Are those requirements being upheld in the interrogation camps?

These captives are not prisoners of war. They are "unlawful combatants."

Meaning they can be held for an indefinite period under inhumane conditions, without access to legal counsel?

The conditions are better than they'd get in their own countries.

Which countries are those? The detainees include Arab Muslims, non-Arab Muslims, Europeans, Australians, South Asians...

I don't know where you've gotten your information. The nationality of the captives is classified.

The Geneva Conventions require that prisoners of war be permitted seven hours sleep a day. Are the 900-odd prisoners of war at Guantánamo Bay permitted seven hours of sleep a day?

I'll tell you one more time that the captives are not technically prisoners of war. They are unlawful combatants. They get as much sleep as they need to get.

Raw

Engineering triumphs like the raw sewage project were just what the US Congress had in mind when it appropriated many billions of dollars to rebuild Iraq.

After having appropriated many billions of dollars to destroy Iraq.

The hope in Congress and throughout America was that major lifestyle improvements such as the pilot sewage project would go some way toward convincing skeptical Iraqis of America's good will.

It is purely for reasons of security that the project has remained secret.

Bechtel officials say the engineering breakthrough occurred in a particularly treacherous part of Baghdad where any publicity could make the project a target for suicide bombers.

"This is the first sewage treatment in Baghdad in 30 years and we can't even get the word out," lamented one American project engineer.

To the suggestion that publicity could lead to sabotage and suicide bombings, the engineer, grinning ruefully, replied:

"Guess what—we're getting our butts bombed anyway."

Just two days before, he said, terrorist insurgents had lobbed a concussion grenade at a Humvee carrying an American computer engineer who was attempting to establish an electronic link among each of the three huge sewage treatment plants being rehabilitated in Baghdad.

Three of the computer engineer's fingers on his left hand were blown away, which means that he'll have a difficult time gripping a cue stick in the officer's club.

Cooked

Our understanding is that the main interrogation area in Guantánamo Bay, where a majority of the detainees are held, is an abandoned aircraft hangar brightly—almost blindingly—lit. Ear-splitting noise, like car alarms, or jackhammers, erupt day and night at uneven intervals, without warning. How can the detainees sleep through that?

If you're tired enough you sleep.

The interrogation sessions go on around-the-clock, conducted by serial teams of what you call interrogators. Individual sessions sometimes extend for months. The detainee is naked and manacled and his hooded head is chained to the ceiling. Is that true?

Is what true?

That the naked, hooded, manacled, chained-to-the-ceiling detainee is interrogated around the clock?

Chaining the captive to the ceiling of an aircraft hanger would take a whole lot of chain, wouldn't it? We try to get the captive to talk in order to save lives. Make sure we don't have another 9/11. This isn't a game we're playing.

Raw

Raw sewage processing plants are hard to conceal, a fact that complicates the effort to keep them secret from those intent on destroying them.

It is true that sewage plants tend to be in the boondocks.

Then again, in a desert country like Iraq, overpopulated with Shias, Sunnis, Kurds, camels, nomads, thousands of feral dogs, and countless vermin, there really are no boondocks as such.

Except for the massive tanks of anaerobic bacteria that process the raw sludge in the pilot plant, few of the industrial sewage-project structures extend above the perimeter stone walls, making the processing plants as little visible and well-protected as possible.

To date, Congress has set aside $60 billion for rebuilding Iraq's physical infrastructure, including electrical, water, sewage, oil, transportation and security installations.

Cooked

The interrogation-related restraints and deprivations you employ include somatic, visual, aural, mental, of course—

It's all well within the lexicon of the Geneva protocols. Which, I emphasize is, on our side, voluntary, since these captives are not technically prisoners of war. They are unlawful combatants.

Meaning what? No safeguards?

We employ all the means in our possession. That is our charge. You wage a war against the captive's resistance at every level to show him that he is wrong. That his ideology is bad and sad and not connected to any true religion or civilized discursive system.

You and your fellow interrogators are sufficiently familiar with these bad and sad ideologies to evaluate their merit? You can, for example, distinguish between a Shia, a Sunni and a Kurd?

We are trained.

By whom?

Experts in the field.

Raw

In a vast, overpopulated desert county, water is lifeblood, so properly functioning raw sewage plants are an absolute necessity.

Sirhan Abdul Sirhan (not his real name), 69, a civil engineer whose mind is an encyclopedia of minutiae on the maddeningly intricate Baghdad sewer system, which he has worked on for four decades, said in an interview at an undisclosed location that there existed more than 6,000 miles of sewer lines, nearly all of which were severely overstressed or actually falling apart.

Rusted or inoperative mechanical parts receive five thousand times more waste than they were designed for, Sirhan said, which produce the fetid tributaries of raw sewage that course through virtually every Baghdad city street.

Moreover, under the tyrant Saddam Hussein, repairs were rare, partial and capricious and always profited Saddam, his mistresses, his family, or the high command of his republican guard.

Those crumbling 6,000 miles of sewer lines feed Baghdad's three massive sewage plants, which have fared even worse than the sewer lines.

In the last two decades the plants became so degraded that Iraqi sewage workers began to divert the raw sewage and pump it into the Tigris with no treatment whatever.

Then, during and after the American-led invasion last year, the sewage plants were looted to the ground by self-destructing Iraqis.

Left behind were graveyards of stinking sludge and gutted buildings.

Initial work to clean them up, largely with shovels and wheelbarrows, commenced late last year.

Iraqis, with their headscarves pulled down over their noses, were commissioned to perform the revolting cleanup under the supervision of the US Army corps of engineers.

Cooked

Our understanding is that there is a very high incidence of suicide in the interment camps. What happens if one of your captives dies either by suicide or as a result of your interrogation?

Those sorts of deaths are rare despite what you've heard. But if it happens and the captive is Muslim, we bury him with his head facing Mecca. Some of this is Geneva Convention, but mostly it's just doing the right thing.

What about sexual defilement? How rare is that?

What do you mean?

Forcing Muslim male and even female detainees to strip naked and to have them perform or simulate sexual acts. With American guards fondling and groping the naked prisoners.

Never happened. Those are lies broadcast by the liberal media. By the European antagonists of America.

And the photos and videos of Abu Ghraib? They were taken by American soldiers on duty in that prison.

Raw

Inside the pilot sewage processing plant, modernized and virtually transformed by the Army corps of engineers under the supervision of Bechtel, the huge clarification tanks have been made ready for sewage.

New filtration screens are fitted into place and electronic-operated pumps are lifting sample sewer water into the air for its trip through the system.

Though impressive, in principle, the plant is not actually treating raw sewage.

The reason, a Bechtel official explained, is that efficient raw sewage treatment means the three plants have to work in concert, and the other two plants are in sectors of Baghdad too dangerous in which to do sustained work.

Nonetheless, this reporter managed to wangle permission from Bechtel to visit one of the other beleaguered plants on the following afternoon.

With Bechtel's intercession and under specified conditions, the First Cavalry Division transported the reporter in a heavily armed four-vehicle convoy.

The conditions were that the reporter neither take photographs nor name names.

Cooked

Those photos and videos were faked. That will come out in due course.

Who faked them?

That I can't say here. But why be surprised. The technology to falsify those sorts of photos and video is easily available, and America has lots of enemies.

What is it about America that has produced so many enemies?

Our courage to do the right thing regardless of cost.

Does the right thing include snatching non-combatant Iraqis from the streets, including women and adolescent boys, transporting them to Guantánamo and interrogating them in isolation for a year, two years?

Raw

Inside the run-down sewage processing plant in an even more treacherous sector of Baghdad, under the unrelenting sun, was a scene out of Kafka: a Kurdish site manager with a cleft palate who did not speak either English or Arabic; Iraqi technicians with identical black mustaches and strict orders not to show anyone the treated sewage without formal permission; and a compound mostly deserted except for low-level staff members, managers, a few engineers, and about a dozen pathetic starving dogs, all of which were brown.

Gray-brown sludge spilled over a ledge in a clarification pond above scum-covered holding pools converging at three concrete canals in a corner of the site.

There, near an empty guard tower and some sparse plants called *koot*, was, at last, a weird but palpable glint of hope in the undisclosed outskirts of this miserable city: treated sewage, swirling around a corner and out of sight into a pair of mismatched tunnels en-route to the Tigris.

Cooked

Interrogation is not an exact science, okay? Occasionally a mistake of one kind or another will be made. Trust me, for every captive that's died or that we've had to maybe bear down on a little bit we've managed to save many thousands of American lives through the information we've extracted.

Trust you? Born and bred in Texarkana, local cop-turned-official torturer, slick-talking corporate patriot eager to launch yet another genocide on behalf of hyper-morality and the power-meisters.

What does Texarkana have to do with anything?

**

As someone who believes Jesus can be seen even in the unwashed faces of those living in Manhattan's deserted storefronts and sewers, Police Officer Manuel Peña claims he obeyed a higher authority when he refused to arrest a homeless man on Christmas Eve, 2003.

Unfortunately for Officer Peña on the beat there isn't any higher authority than the Mayor of New York, and after fielding thousands of complaints from wealthy residents and politicians, the Mayor decreed that a zero tolerance policy be set in place for the homeless. No exceptions. It was up to the police commissioner to see that that decree was implemented.

The result is that the non-compliant cop is now confronted with a departmental trial that could very well cost him his livelihood. In an interview with Rupert Murdoch's *New York Post*, headlined **Compassionate Cop Bucks System**, Officer Peña, 38, described himself as a religious person who was committed to carrying out his job effectively but also with compassion, especially for the poorest of the poor, with whom he came into contact on a daily basis.

After two years of swing shifts patrolling the Port Authority Bus Terminal near Times Square, the compassionate cop put in for a transfer to the Homeless Outreach Unit, which he saw as a way to help those at the very bottom of the food chain. The transfer was approved. As Officer Peña, on his new beat, ventured deeper into the tunnels and sewers, he found to his astonishment humans living like spiders. Sewer pipes, cardboard cartons, industrial rope and cord, newspaper, umbrellas, and other discarded items were used—often ingeniously—to fashion shelters of various kind, which were then decorated with plants, religious objects and family portraits. The primary entrance to the largest series of sewers, the officer said, is, ironically, less than ten feet south of the entrance to the celebrated Waldorf Astoria on Park Avenue. There, twenty to approximately fifty feet underground, spreading both south and east, he found a small army of homeless humans, mostly male, but including females and children, living like trolls beneath the functioning world.

"Their will to live and the resourcefulness with which they went about it amazed me," the compassionate cop said. Rather than arrest, he befriended a number of them and even supplied them with food, clothing and other necessities. He provided this service privately, he said, without making a report or filling out "all the usual bureaucratic forms." Many of the men were veterans of the Vietnam War and some younger men and a few women claimed to be veterans of the Gulf War in 1991 who'd become very ill with the Gulf War Syndrome, from which they still suffered.

"The thing is, I didn't see them as homeless," Officer Peña said. "I saw them as people down on their luck. Let's face it, this is a real hard city to live in if you don't have big money. A whole lot of people, no matter how hard they work, if they get sick and are out of the job for a month, are going to find themselves in the street."

The compassionate cop was doing his duty as he saw fit for about a year and a half, until November 2003, when the Mayor's office finished processing the complaints from wealthy residents and the politicians they'd enlisted and passed down the zero tolerance directive. Cops were instructed to ask the homeless if they wanted to go to a shelter. If the homeless refused and didn't have a legal ID, they were arrested and carted away to one of the large holding tanks.

Officer Peña said tensions arose in late December when his superiors noted that his "arrest chart" was much less filled than expected. On Christmas eve, 2003, he was ordered to go to the Port Authority Bus Terminal where he'd had his former beat and question the homeless on the second tier.

With his sergeant looking over his shoulder, the compassionate cop was told to wake up an old man sleeping soundly under one of the commuter benches. Officer Peña did that, and it took some time for the old man to comprehend that he was asked to display identification. When he couldn't produce a valid ID Officer Peña asked him if he wanted to go to a homeless shelter, and again the old man didn't understand him. But instead of arresting him, the compassionate cop touched his shoulder affectionately and moved back. It was left for the sergeant to arrest the old homeless man and cart him away.

"I couldn't arrest him," Officer Peña explained. "It was Christmas Eve. He was a very old man. He was better off where he was at, in my opinion, than in a cramped holding tank with seventy other homeless men." But to the police department the issue is cut and dried: "The officer disobeyed a lawful order from his superior," said Carol Steen-Canaday, the deputy commissioner for public information. "That is a serious breach of duty. To make an exception for this officer would be incorrect and illegal. Now he has to stand trial like any other disobeying officer. The exact penalty will be decided after the trial. That's the way it is done in a democracy."

Officer Peña has already been suspended from the force without pay for fifty-five days as he awaits trial. His wife, Hortensia, and their four children are frightened about the future. The compassionate cop claims he himself isn't frightened, just uneasy on his family's behalf.

Officer Peña explained that he was not against arresting homeless people if they were criminals or potentially violent, but that there was, to him, a big difference between a person down on his luck and a criminal. The reason he joined the Homeless Outreach Unit to begin with was in the Christian spirit of serving those most in need. "To me, and to many Christians, that is the most noble thing any human can do. That's what my wife and I both believe and that is what we have tried to teach our children."

Nevertheless, Officer Peña now says that if faced with the same situation, he would have "complied with the sergeant's orders." Not that he believed arresting the old homeless man was the right thing to do, but simply to "spare my wife and children any more suffering."

Things To Do
During Time of War

Wednesday, six-fifty a.m.

Clock-radio.

Wakened out of a dream.

Your father—long dead—is in it, and you as a child.

Also a blue guitar, or maybe a banjo.

You suppress the dream, shuffle to the machine.

Access email.

104 messages, 97 of them SPAM.

(You installed an anti-SPAM filter but the cyber-terrorists are always a step ahead).

Delete SPAM.

Post an email message.

Post another.

Post another.

Send a fax.

Consult electronic address book.

Send another fax.

Shuffle into the kitchen.

Switch on the miniature kitchen TV.

Stock quotations from major markets worldwide.

Charts, graphs, visuals.

Experts' commentary.

Part and parcel of the global economy.

Does global mean totalitarian?

It would be cynical to think "yes."
Well, cynics sit at their computers and go to the bathroom.
They salute the flag and masturbate.
They have mothers and fathers like everyone else.
You grind your beans.
Brewing coffee.
Add vanilla.
Designer coffee, low-carb toast, buttered.
They claim now that fat's all right.
Swallow your vitamin packet with papaya juice.
Recommended for digestion.
Switch off the TV.
Coffee refill.
Carry the mug of coffee to your machine.
Delete SPAM.
Asleep, awake, it multiplies like cancer.
Post another email message.
Scan pertinent web sites.
Check the weather online.
Heat, smog.
What else can it be?
Scan the LA Times online.
The wars they are a-spreading.
Disclosure of torture in international prisons.
Americans no less.
The business sector is booming.
Oil futures up, dollar steady, unemployment rising.
No, it's *employment* that is rising.
Sorry about that.
War insures investment hence insures the peace.
Afghanistan, Pakistan, Iraq, Palestine, Saudi Arabia, Syria, the
Koreas, Indonesia, Horn of Africa, Sudan, Yemen, Colombia,
Venezuela, Cuba...

What's up with Cuba?

Cuba post-millennium encourages foreign investment.

With all of its setbacks, it's still a fairy tale Caribbean isle with much to offer in the tourist sectors especially.

Born-again Cuban capitalists shuffle their feet, smoke restlessly in the wings, waiting for Fidel to finally croak.

Neither the FBI nor the CIA could off him, but now his beard has turned white.

Dude has to drop dead sometime.

Scan the LA Times sports section online: cheerleading, skate-boarding, water-skiing, water-skateboarding, bungee jumping, shark hunting with sharpened dildos, beach volleyball, bowling for fat people, "world series of poker" from Las Vegas, midgets racing monster trucks, French-kissing piranha, extreme suicide...

Fiercely competitive, every one of them.

Sip your coffee.

Exit email.

Put your machine to sleep.

Shower, shave, floss, brush, apply cologne, insert contacts.

Boxers, white tee, socks, shirt, tie, suit, shoes.

Wallet, keys, cellphone, American flag lapel pin, ID nametag, black leather briefcase.

Clip the nametag to your lapel.

Out of the condo, into the garage.

Into your new white SUV.

Set your briefcase on the passenger seat.

Your new SUV is white like the winning side in the ongoing war against terrorism.

Ongoing because the war will not cease until the white hats impose their will.

Such is the price of democracy.

Smell the spanking-new leather upholstery of your new SUV.

Open the garage door with your remote.

Start the potent, sweet engine and the radio comes on.

Today, it turns out, is Orange Alert day.

So declares Old Squarejaw, chief of Homeland Security.

Al-Qaeda operatives with identical black mustaches and explosives taped to their bodies have slipped across the borders.

Likely through Mexico.

Report any and all suspicious humans.

You turn off the radio and insert a CD.

Hook your cellphone on the dash.

Turn on the A.C.

Off to the office.

Receive a call on your cell in your white SUV.

Make a call on your cell in your white SUV.

Consult your electronic phone book.

Make another call.

Accelerate to 80.

Coasting.

Speed kills, but not in your white SUV.

Rides like a sharp knife cutting through butter.

Change lanes on the freeway.

Mutter at the other drivers.

Mentally compare other SUVs on the freeway with your own.

Fast-forward the CD.

A swarthy subhuman with a black mustache pulls alongside you in his black Citroën sedan, makes agitated gestures, then lowers his window and shoots you in the head with his Beretta semi-automatic.

You're dead so you don't make it to the office.

Actually you don't die, you aren't shot, you make it to the office.

Turn into the underground lot.

Park in your middle manager slot.

Turn off the A.C.

Employ your secure ID to enter the building.

Employ your secure ID to enter your sector.

In your office you set your black briefcase on your desk.

Framed photo of your adolescent daughter from your divorced marriage on your desk.

Girl's name is Holly.

Divorced wife's name is **money-lust demon from the nether regions**.

Inventory the messages on your office phone.

Scan the eleven faxes, eight of them SPAM.

Remove your suit jacket and hang it on the coat hanger.

Your next promotion will mean a larger office and small closet to hang your suit jacket in.

If you're lucky.

Move to the computer terminal alongside your desk and access your email.

119 messages, 103 of them SPAM.

Delete the SPAM.

Post eleven messages.

Send three faxes.

Make six phone calls from your cell while sitting at the terminal.

Access CNN news online.

Another suicide bombing, another helicopter gunship attack, more torture uncovered, another savage beheading, oil prices rising steeply thanks to the Arab oil cartel.

Orange Alert will continue at least through the weekend.

Send for coffee, double latte from Starbucks.

Phone buzzes, meeting at eleven in the boardroom.

Latte arrives.

More phone and online business.

At the meeting a VP with a bad hair weave addresses the managers.

Earnings are up this quarter but they could do better, must do better. Or else.

"Or else" implied not spoken.

Not unlike the official orders to "interrogate with firmness."

Sanitized way of saying "torture the gooks."

The army reserve drones called up to serve in Iraq prisons understand.

The national guard drones called up to serve in Iraq prisons understand.

After the boardroom meeting, a hurried buffet lunch in the cafeteria downstairs.

Back at the office, more calls, online contacts, faxes, another meeting, more coffee.

Decaf this time.

You're back in the white SUV, on the freeway, 6:12 pm, gridlock.

Receiving calls, making calls, switching lanes, muttering at other drivers.

A swarthy subhuman with a black mustache pulls alongside you in his black Citroën sedan, makes agitated gestures, then lowers his window and shoots you in the head with his Beretta semi-automatic.

This time you do die.

Nonetheless you return to your condo at 7:18, pull into the garage.

Inside at your computer are 111 messages, 103 of them SPAM.

Eight faxes, six of them SPAM

8:05 p.m.

Enema time.

Warm water, not hot.

Mix with a teaspoon of chamomile tea.

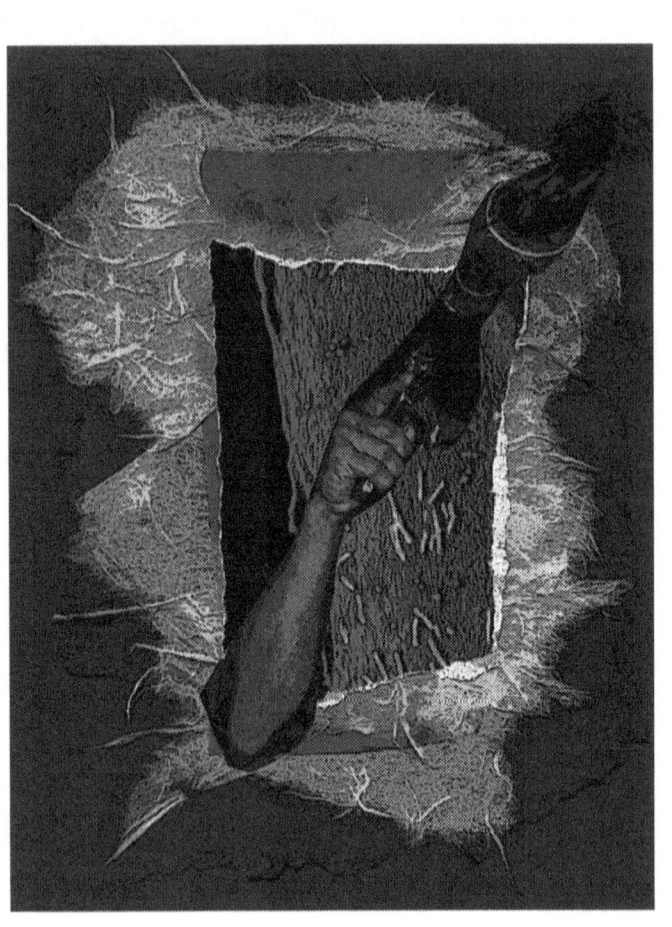

Terrorchildren

It was the day after 9/11 and all over the Third World the children woke up crying. In Hyderabad and Islamabad, in East Timor and Dacca, in Dar es Salaam and Qena, in Kano and Baghdad. In thousands of cities, villages, hamlets, pueblos, kraals, backwaters the children woke up crying.

When Heather Gosling came up with the idea of using weeds as weapons in the war against terror, she figured most people would call it a joke.

But the federal government didn't laugh.

Now, armed with a $1.5 million dollar grant from the Pentagon, the demure, middle-aged Texas Lutheran College biologist is trying to genetically engineer plants to change color rapidly when they sense a toxic biological or chemical agent.

If Dr. Gosling's plan works, the technology could be used to turn forest oaks, backyard shrubs, pond algae, even festooned Christmas trees into sentinels in the war against terrorism.

Ironically, the most sensitive houseplant to toxic agents is arguably the most common, the philodendron, especially *Philodendron domesticum.*

Gosling explained her anti-terror experiments this way: "A lot of us scientists started thinking differently after 9/11.

"More patriotically, you might say."

However, when she ran her idea by the Defense Department, she didn't know what to expect.

But Defense Department Secretary Donald Rumsfeld's assistant in charge of "private sector interface grants," Benton "Buzz" Harrier, proved receptive.

As Gosling recounts the story in her just-released book, *Houseplants Against Terror* (American Enterprise, $38), "Buzz Harrier, behind his outsized Pentagon steel and glass desk, poured himself some black coffee from his old-fashioned Sharper Image thermos, regarded me narrowly through his gun-shooter gray eyes, took a long sip, set down his red, white and blue mug, then said in his quiet, Yale-by-way-of-North Carolina tenor:

"'Shoot, let's give it a trah, because if it does work, it could make a heckuva difference in our war against terrorism.'"

Under the terms of Gosling's grant, Buzz Harrier gave her 18 months to figure out how to make plants tattle on terrorists.

In *Houseplants Against Terror*, which has already climbed to number 9 on the USA Today Best Seller list, Gosling spells out certain fascinating details of her scientific experiments.

For example, if one of her sentinel plants signals a deadly nerve agent such as sarin, it would probably be too late to prevent people in the vicinity from dying horribly of sarin poisoning.

But if her plant signals anthrax, smallpox or plague, most non-moronic Americans would know they were exposed before displaying symptoms.

Which would allow them ample time to ingest potent FDA-approved antibiotics and duct-tape themselves into their condos with their significant other, low-carb snacks, bible, cellphone, TV and Internet.

Dr. Gosling explains in her book that she is not permitted by law to employ real biological and chemical terrorist agents in her experiments, which are aimed at causing the rapid breakdown of chlorophyll.

Instead she uses the hormone estrogen because it prompts the "de-greening circuit" in plants.

Which has provoked such good-natured jibes from her colleagues as:

"Estrogen could be a poisonous terrorist agent."

"Beware of menopausal women bearing government grants!"

Dr. Gosling concludes her volume with the bold prediction that "one day in the not too distant future, everyone in America, irrespective of race, religion or gender, will be able to use a houseplant such as the familiar *Philodendron domesticum* both as beautification and as an early-warning system to signal a terrorist attack.

"God willing."

In actuality, Heather Gosling's Texas Lutheran laboratory is just one among scores of high-tech labs springing up across the country where scientists and entrepreneurs are furiously competing to invent products that will help the government respond to another terrorist attack.

And, of course, reap the handsome rewards, since not only are the government grants bountiful, those dollars generate yet more dollars from the private sector, which tends to jump on the *au courant* capitalist band-wagon.

This is referred to as money following money.

It was the day before 9/11 and throughout the Third World the children woke up crying. In Kuala Lumpur and Kandahar, in Phnom Penh and El Karak and Mogadishu and Gaza. And in the Third World that exists in the First World—the margins and inner cities, the invisible ghettoes and reservations stretching from the Big Apple to the Golden State, up and down the coasts—the invisible children woke up crying.

Meanwhile, in Nutley, New Jersey, a corporate entomologist named Poorwill is trapping beetles, crickets, bees and moths to determine whether they can be used as environmental monitors of a biological or chemical attack.

In Needles, California, free-lance scientist-entrepreneur, Joe Ray Goldeneye (he's Mohave Indian on his father's side), has worked since the day after 9/11 to see whether insects can deliver information about hazardous or deadly agents in the soil, on the ground or in the air.

Funded by a $1.3 million Pentagon grant, Goldeneye uses black lights, super glue and customized traps to collect more than 17 species of bugs.

The bugs are "like little sponges or dust mops," Goldeneye explains.

If security officials suspect that a toxic agent has been released into, say, a shopping mall or a theme park, they "deploy the bugs to crawl and fly around the suspected area, picking up samples, then collect the bugs for testing."

For routine monitoring, the bugs could serve as a crucial part of a "24/7 sampling scheme."

In Davenport, Iowa, a high-tech company called Full Court Press, with liberal funding from the illiberal Pentagon, is attempting to invent an inexpensive device that would isolate DNA from any infectious disease and instantly diagnose it.

If it functions as drawn up, emergency workers, medical technicians and hospitals could figure out fast whether a human, food or soft drink has been infected and identify the infectious toxin.

Today, in terms of bio-detection, "we're in the stone age," asserts Full Court Press founder L. Casey Longspur.

"You go to a doctor's office, they take a sample of urine or blood, and you hang in there for a week biting your knuckles, waiting for the results.

"That's not the way it should be."

Longspur's eyes gloss over when he relates his dream: "To see my Full Court Press bio-detector in post offices, water treatment plants, ball parks, shopping malls, fitness centers and places of worship... anywhere a biohazard could be released."

Many of these efforts sound like they belong in a science-fiction movie.

But they are all real-time, cutting-edge projects lavishly funded by government $$$.

Security officials acknowledge that probably most of the projects won't pan out, but they maintain that it is a risk worth taking even if only a single project turns into a useful addition to the ongoing war on terror.

To date, the vast majority of these projects have been funded by the Defense Department.

But after having tightened security at the nation's borders and airports and established a system of non-stop surveillance of American citizens, both the Justice Department and the Department of Homeland Security are now funding projects deemed worthy and have set aside 3 billion dollars for that purpose.

Why not? It's the same money they've stripped from social services to the aged and indigent, from the schools and inner cities, from the docile, eroded middle class.

"We aim to attract the very best minds from the private sectors and the academic community and get them working on high-stakes, high-security projects," Homeland Security Secretary Tom Ridge declared in a recent speech marking the department's 200-day anniversary.

Yesterday, in Jerusalem, a 17-year-old Palestinian girl, wired with explosives, exchanged a lingering look with a 17-year-old Israeli girl as she was boarding a bus to go to school. Then the Palestinian girl boarded the same bus and detonated, killing both herself, the Israeli girl, nineteen passengers and the bus driver.

Many of the projects the department has funded are classified so that terrorists can't penetrate our technologies and subvert them.

But other projects are part of the public record.

What follows is the Department of Homeland Security's current (non-classified) wish list, which you can also find on their official web site: www.HomeSec.gov.

An electronic device that could help border and airport-security workers profile folks who are up to no good.

When security agents in any department are asked why they search certain cars or question certain passengers, they usually can't pinpoint what made them wary, beyond the fact that the individual was black or brown and wore a do-rag.

So Homeland Security is appealing to universities and corporate think tanks to devise technology that will mark suspects by their physiological responses to interrogation.

Scientists know, for example, that blood rushes to the eye muscles of someone who is lying, the suspect tends to stammer, his ears redden (if he is Caucasian), his nose gets longer by degree, and he displays other "thermal signatures" that signify evil doing or at least complicity in a terrorist activity.

But, under law, security agents need definitive proof to jail and torture a suspect, otherwise the evidence they present in court, often at considerable cost to the taxpayer, will likely be inadmissible

Self-decontamination kits that could be given to victims of a chemical attack.

The kits must be easy to open without tools and include a decontaminant that is safe to use on skin, wounds and mucus membranes.

The instruction manual should not exceed 150 pages, should be accessible to the sight-impaired, and the kit, including DVD, should cost no more than $39.95, plus postage.

Advanced technology to protect commercial and corporate aircraft from shoulder-fired missiles during takeoffs and landings. These primitive but occasionally deadly weapons are favored by technology-challenged, non-Caucasian terrorists.

The anti-terrorist technology should be practical in terms of the cost of retrofitting aircraft and must contain a warning system for both ground operators and pilots.

The system must also consider the impact of missile-related collateral damage to areas surrounding commercial airports.

A sonar-based sea mine detection system that can search harbors, channels and rivers for anti-personnel mines or other "threat-objects" that have been secreted in the water.

A computer program that would distinguish between African-American suspects who are patriotic Americans, as they claim, and pseudo-patriots who secretly sympathize with Islamic terrorists for reasons of race, religion or generalized bitterness.

Hundreds of unsolicited proposals already have made their way to homeland security officials in recent months from corporations, think tanks, reformed hackers, and universities eager to win grants and contracts.

The department's grants administrator Phoebe S. Groundchat was at an event with Homeland Security head Tom Ridge recently when, in Groundchat's words, "this nerdy guy with thick glasses, smelling real strong of perspiration, walked up to me with a manila envelope and said: 'I'm a post-9/11 tech looking for a fat pay-day.

"'Can you make sure this gets into the right hands?'"

Groundchat assures concerned Americans that the Department of Homeland Security already employs state-of-the-art technology for bomb detection, disease tracking and cybersecurity.

But, as Groundchat puts it, "With vermin-terrorists becoming more and more cunning, heck, we can always build a better mousetrap."

It was the day before and the day after 9/11 and throughout the Third World the children woke up crying. In Kuala Lumpur and Kandahar, in Phnom Penh and El Karak and Mogadishu and Kano and Gaza. And in the Third World that exists in the First World—the margins and inner cities, the invisible ghettoes and reservations stretching from New York to the Golden State, up and down the coasts—the unheard children woke up crying.

Monk & Suicide Bomber

Do you pray?

Earnestly.
Avidly.

For whom do you pray?

For the long-suffering, the dispossessed.
Mothers of murdered children.
The family whose small house is exploded because the son is suspected of defending his people with stones.
The martyrs themselves.

You pray for the martyrs?

I do.

Aren't the martyrs already assured of ample reward in the next world?

I pray for them nonetheless.

[Pause]

What of the dispossessed among your victims?
Do your prayers include them?

I do not understand.

Your bombs kill children, mothers.
Their violent, untimely deaths leave those who love them dispos-
sessed. True?

Undoubtedly.

But they are not in your prayers?

No.
They are, collectively, our sworn enemy.
I cannot think of them as individuals.
To do so would prevent me from my primary obligation which is to
liberate our people from the enemy's long and brutal oppression.
To protect the innocent.

[Pause]

Are there not those among your sworn enemies who are innocent?

No.
The brutal context will not permit it.

Do you believe that?

I must.

Like yourself, your enemy professes to be God-fearing.
Even if their God is different.
Your enemy, then, also prays.
Is it possible that some among them pray for you?

For me?

For you and your people.
Do some among your sworn enemy pray for the very people that their government oppresses and murders?

It is possible, I suppose.
I doubt it.
Well, it could be that a minuscule number among them recognize their barbarity and feel guilt but are unable to do anything practical about it because of their government's iron fist.

So they pray.

They pray for their own expiation.
Where nobody can hear them.
What does it matter?
When it is a country's undisguised policy to exterminate or at the very least dispossess an entire nation, of what use are a hundred people who profess to be against genocide?
How prepared were the Nazi holocaust victims to forgive those Germans who claimed they disapproved of their country's genocide, but were, they insisted, impotent to modify it?

[Pause]

The fact is our own situation has become more grave, not less.
Rather than extermination or existing under their brutal occupation, we have chosen our own deaths.

You refer to the suicide bombings?
Exploding school busses.
Commercial aircraft.

Concealing bombs in straw baskets and blowing up restaurants where working people come to eat and have a cup of coffee.

Let us have their weapons technology.
Their planes and tanks and missiles, their helicopter gunships.
Their depleted uranium which poison our people and our crops.
We will exchange them our children's stones.
Our donkey carts.
Our straw baskets with home-made bombs inside them.
We will then bomb their school busses and working class restaurants from above the cloud cover so that we cannot hear the screams.

As they, with their advanced weapons technology, do?

Yes.

Whereas you defend yourself the only way you—a poor country—can.
Suicide bombing.

Yes.

You trust the leaders on your side who select the enemy targets and arm the suicide bombers?

Implicitly.
Our leaders lead at our behest.
They are God-fearing.
Committed solely to our people's welfare.

[Pause]

Whose faces do I see plastered on the battered walls?

Those are our fighters, our martyrs.

I see faces of children.
Teenage girls.

Our young freedom fighters.
They believed in peace when there were legitimate hopes for peace.
When those hopes were smashed the only honorable option left was to sacrifice their lives for their people.
With God's grace.

I read where one of your leaders said that "the body of the exploding martyr has the fine odor of musk."
Is that an appropriate remark to make to children who are perhaps not disposed to murder themselves and others?

I will not pass judgment on what our leaders are reputed to have said.

[Pause]

Will your people and their people ever be able to live side-by-side?

That is a question you should address to them.
I used to believe-or wanted to believe-that it was possible.
Now I cannot say.
In truth I think it is not possible.
To them we are contemptible.
You have seen those photographs and videotapes of torture the torturers themselves took?

Yes.

How their soldiers not only tormented but degraded their prisoners.

Then admitted that the majority of those prisoners were not even combatants.

Merely Muslims snatched off the streets.

To the colonizers it does not matter, torture one, murder another.

Bomb our milk factories, bomb our holy shrines.

To them it is the same.

Collateral damage.

You can understand, then, that to us they are the most savage of colonizers.

[Pause]

We wish to live in peace.

Worship God and try, with God's grace, to elevate our lives and actions.

But we will not turn the other cheek.

That is the advice of the other God, which in any case is never heeded.

Our God demands that we combat to the death their industry of extermination.

My understanding is that your God forbids the murder of the innocent and forbids suicide under any conditions.

I also understood your God to forbid the murder of humans or animals by fire, which would proscribe suicide bombings.

Your understanding is disputable.

Extraordinary conditions demand extraordinary measures.

If we stand pat we are genocided or dispossessed from our land, our burying grounds, our holy sanctuaries.

We are a poor people.

If we fight conventionally we cannot compete with their advanced weaponry.

Thus we fight back any way we can.

Which, in our understanding, is what the holy books counsel.

If they turn our ancestral land into a black hole, they will be sucked into the blackness along with their intended victims, you can be certain.

[Pause]

Yourself, you are a priest?

I am a Buddhist monk.

I recall Mahatma Gandhi being asked how he would counsel the Jews to respond as they were led to the gas.

His answer was that they must look their executioner in the eye.

Perhaps he was thinking of the British.

In any event his response was misinformed.

You look a Nazi in the eye and he plucks it out of your head.

You have to know your enemy.

Our enemy is implacable.

We must then use any and all means at our disposal to resist and if need be to eradicate them.

I see.

[Pause]

Gandhi was Hindu or Buddhist?

Hindu.

Didn't your Buddhists set themselves on fire during the Americans' violent occupation of Vietnam?

Yes, a number of Buddhists: monks, nuns and laypeople, immolated themselves.
It did not appear to affect the immediate situation.
Individual suicide is not the same as suicide bombing.

You approve, then, of individual suicide?

As a tactic against war or occupation, it may in certain instances effect change.
As Gandhi did in his hunger fasts, which would have become suicide, had the British not relented.

Our enemy is not British.

No.

How, then, would you have us respond?

[Pause]

Call for a cease fire.
Enlist the mediation of outside countries who have no stake in the war.
Reopen discussion with the other side.
Pray for the innocent and even the non-innocent on either side.
Do not lose faith.

Will you offer this same counsel to the other side?

If they are willing to listen, yes.

And if that initiative, however well-intentioned, amounts to nothing?
As similar initiatives have amounted to nothing?

What then?
What would you counsel then?

[Silence]

*Terror-Dot-Gov is in good part derived from "news" both online and off. I have reconstituted reports and articles from a number of sources, including Le Monde, Le Figaro, The Guardian, The Independent, BBC News Online, The New York Times, The LA Times, Z-Net, and the San Francisco Chronicle.

**The information on depleted uranium in "Terror Couture" is drawn primarily from the investigations of Dai Williams and Doug Rokke. See www.eoslifework.co.uk and www.wired.com/news/conflict

***The details of the murder of Mustafa Hussein in "Baghdad Barbershop" are closely derived from Robert Fisk's impassioned article, "The Ghosts of Uday and Qusay," in The Independent, August 6, 2003. Another portion of "Baghdad Barbershop" is drawn from a New York Times article on July 24, 2003. The improvisations which constitute the core of the "docufiction" suggest virtually opposite conclusions from the Times.

About the Author

Harold Jaffe is the author of nine fiction (or "docufiction") collections and three novels, including *Beasts*, *Madonna and Other Spectacles*, *Straight Razor*, *False Positive*, and *15 Serial Killers*. His fiction has been anthologized in *Pushcart Prize*, *Best American Stories*, *Best of American Humor*, *Storming the Reality Studio*, *American Made*, *Avant Pop: Fiction for a Daydreaming Nation*, *After Yesterday's Crash*, and elsewhere. His writings have been translated into German, Japanese, Spanish, Italian, French, Polish, and Czech. Jaffe is editor-in-chief of *Fiction International*.